I0608364

PIONEER DELIGHT

THE O'ROURKE FAMILY MONTANA SAGA

BOOK NINE

RAMONA FLIGHTNER

GRIZZLY DAMSEL PUBLISHING

Copyright © 2022 by Ramona Flightner

All rights reserved. No portion of this book may be reproduced in any form or by any electronic or mechanical means including information storage and retrieval systems – except in the case of brief quotations in articles or reviews – without permission in writing from its publisher, Ramona Flightner and Grizzly Damsel Publishing. Copyright protection extends to all excerpts and previews by this author included in this book.

This novel is a work of fiction. Names, characters, businesses, places, events and incidents are either the products of the author's imagination or used in a fictitious manner. Any resemblance to actual persons, living or dead, or actual events is purely coincidental.

All brand names and product names used in this book are trademarks, registered trademarks, or trade names of their respective holders. The author or publisher is not associated with any product or vendor in this book.

Cover design by Jennifer Quinlan.

ABOUT PIONEER DELIGHT

Henrietta Foyle is grateful for the life she's building with the O'Rourkes. Thankful for her second chance, she consoles herself with friendship with the man she secretly loves, Niall O'Rourke. Her best friend, she knows he'll never see her as anything more than dependable Hettie. When she has the chance with another, Hettie faces the hardest choice of her life: abandon her dream or be courageous and fight for her heart's desire.

Niall O'Rourke lives a charmed life working in his family's saloon with his best friend and brother. Life is how he's always dreamed it would be and he hopes it will never change. When his dreams for his future with Hettie are threatened, he realizes he must act, or lose the woman of his dreams forever.

As old ghosts return to threaten their future, will Niall and Hettie be brave or will they risk the love growing between them?

CHAPTER 1

Fort Benton, Montana Territory; June 1873

Niall O'Rourke waved at his younger brothers, Oran and Henri, to quiet them, as they snickered and giggled and poked at each other, while huddled together in a living room corner. "He's coming, and, if you ruin this now, I'll kill you," Niall hissed, although his green eyes shone with affection. Glancing around, grinning, he searched for Hettie, wanting to share this moment with her, but he didn't see her.

Hettie was one of his two best friends, and she lived with his family. She'd arrived in Fort Benton four years ago, when Winnie had returned from her banishment, and now Niall couldn't imagine Hettie not being part of his life. When he thought of Hettie, he was filled with joy. For now he focused on the moment, not wanting to ruin their intricately made plans.

Peeking around the doorjamb, Niall saw Bryan, his youngest brother and the youngest O'Rourke, enter the backdoor with stooped shoulders. Generally Bryan was bursting with energy and always had a ready smile and a tale to tell. Leaning forward, Niall listened as Bryan approached their mum, Mary.

"Where is everyone?" He looked around the empty kitchen that was usually teeming with O'Rourkes at this hour. "I thought ..." He shrugged, and Niall watched Bryan's brave attempt at hiding his disappointment.

"Ah, you know how it is, love," Mary said, with an absent smile. She then ducked her head, lest Bryan saw the mischief in her gaze. She'd protested her part in this scheme, as she had proclaimed herself no actor, but had finally been convinced to play this part. "'Tis a busy summer day, and everyone has more important things to do than sit around, watchin' me cook."

Bryan let out a deep breath, as his shoulders stooped so low that Niall thought they'd soon kiss the floor. "Of course. More important things." He plopped down at the table and sat, staring into space. "I thought ..." He shrugged and shook his head.

Niall looked over his shoulder and shared a concerned glance with Da. Now sixty-one, Seamus O'Rourke was unquestionably the patriarch of the family. Tall, like many of his sons, his hair was more gray than black, and he had many more lines around his striking blue eyes, which he claimed were from the joy his ever-growing family brought him. His wise counsel, unconditional love, and endless supply of encouragement were cherished by all his children. Now Seamus nodded, and everyone stilled, even the youngest O'Rourkes.

Niall looked over his shoulder again, frowning when he failed to see Hettie, before giving his head a little shake and sauntering into the kitchen. He kissed his mum on her cheek and gave her a wink only she could see. He saw the worry in her gaze and wished he could give her an encouraging smile. "Hey, Bryan. How was your day?"

His youngest brother heaved out a sigh and stared at him mournfully, his green eyes shining with sadness. "So boring. No one was around. Every place I went, everyone was gone." He shook his head. "Or busy. Even Mr. Pickens was too busy for a story."

Niall knew that would be the worst torment for Bryan, as he loved a good story more than anything and thrived at making up tall tales to see if his listeners could tell truth from fiction. Niall asked, "I wonder why? It's not like today is a special day or anything." He worked hard not to soothe his brother, when Bryan flinched at Niall's teasingly spoken words.

Bryan bit his lip, his gaze filled with hurt, as he stared at his older brother. After swallowing, he shrugged and muttered, "No, of course it isn't."

Speaking a bit louder than he needed to, Niall said, "Yeah, it's not like it's …" Niall paused as the entire O'Rourke clan and A.J. and Bessie Pickens poured into the kitchen, all shouting and hollering, before screaming at the same time, "Your birthday!" Niall hooted and gave a cheer, laughing at Bryan's shock. He only hoped his baby brother didn't faint dead away at their surprise.

Bryan stood, his mouth wide open, gaping at his family, as he shook his head in disbelief. Tears clung to his long eyelashes, although he tried to blink them away. "You remembered?" Swiping at his flushed cheeks, he stared from one sibling to another and then grunted, as he was pulled into a hug. Oran and Henri were the first to hug him, teasing him and wishing him well all in one breath.

Niall waited his turn, before tugging Bryan into his arms and giving him a huge hug and a soft slap on his shoulder. "Happy eighteenth birthday, baby brother."

"Of course we remembered, lad," Seamus said, as he hauled his boy into his arms and patted him on his back. "'Tisn't every day my youngest becomes a man." Seamus cleared his throat, overcome with his emotions. "I'm proud of you, lad."

Niall scooted away, allowing his huge family time with the birthday boy. Niall knew the family café and saloon had been closed for the evening. Soon they'd head to the café for the private family celebration. With how large the family was now, it was much more comfortable to take over the café than attempt to cram into the kitchen of the big O'Rourke house, although not nearly as cozy.

Niall looked around the family kitchen and smiled. He loved his loud unrestrained family, who unabashedly showed their love and affection for each other. Although not all his siblings shared the same mum *and* dad, only Seamus or Mary, it didn't matter. They were family, united by the love they shared with each other.

He felt a prickling sensation on his neck, and he turned his gaze to the kitchen entrance, smiling when he saw Hettie. His smile quickly transformed into a frown, when he saw her hovering there, rather than joining in the festivities. Didn't she understand she was part of the family? "Hett!" he called out, rushing to her side and pulling on her arm. He laughed when she flushed and batted at his hand. "Come on. You know you're one of us."

He grinned when she giggled, and then she grabbed Bryan close for a hug. After she'd congratulated the birthday boy, Niall waited for her to come stand beside him. They'd been best friends since her arrival in Fort Benton, and he always enjoyed her gentle wit and soft laugh, as they joked and teased their way through meals or long work-days. Everything was easier with Hettie around. He marveled that it had only been four years since she'd arrived and had been adopted into the family, for he couldn't envision a life without her presence.

He didn't know what he'd do without her friendship. He was nearly as close to her as he was to his brother, Lucien, who was only eleven months older than him. However, Lucien had married four years ago—which made Hettie's friendship so much more precious to Niall. As was natural, Lucien had a busy life with his wife, Samantha, and their son, which didn't leave as much time for Niall in Lucien's life.

Niall sighed, as he knew that was how it was supposed to be, but he missed those days when he could spend time with just Lucien. However, looking at his brother, cuddling his exhausted son against his chest, all Niall felt was grateful for all Lucien had.

Thus Niall was thankful for the constancy of Hettie's friendship. He knew he'd be lost without it. Glancing around, he saw his brother Finn, chatting with Eamon, and realized the family hadn't had as grand a celebration as this since Finn and Winnie's wedding party four years ago. Although many birthday celebrations had been had, nothing ever rivaled a wedding celebration, even if it was a belated party, as it had been for Winnie and Finn.

"Congratulations," Hettie murmured, as she sidled up next to Niall. Her golden hair was tied back in a loose knot, and her brandy-colored eyes shone with happiness. "You managed to keep the surprise a surprise. I never thought you'd pull it off, not with Oran and Henri." She giggled when she saw the pack all together.

Although they were older and much bigger now than when they were given the nickname, the three youngest O'Rourkes were still called "the pack" by the family. Oran, Henri, and Bryan were inseparable and did everything together.

"Did you know they'd made a pact when Oran turned eighteen to never lie to each other?" Niall rolled his eyes. "They won't even do a little fib for us. Like keeping this party a secret. So, Dunmore kidnapped the two wee rascals"—he nodded to Oran and Henri—"and got them away from town until just before the party, just so Bryan couldn't ask them any questions."

Hettie held a hand over her mouth, as she stifled a laughing fit. "Oh, it was so much harder than you thought it would be, wasn't it?"

He grinned and sighed with pleasure. "So much harder. I don't know how Da put up with the lot of us."

Her smile softened to see Seamus beaming at his family, as he held Maggie's two-year-old son to his chest. "You're lucky, Niall. He only ever saw the joy of you." She made a small waving motion to encompass all the O'Rourkes present. "Of all of you."

He grinned and bumped his shoulder against hers. "You know what would make this moment perfect?" When she stared up at him, as though expecting him to say something profound, he leaned closer and whispered, "If we'd already eaten the huge meal waiting for us at the café. I'm starving." When she tapped him on his belly, he grunted.

"You're always hungry and sneaking food. Don't think for a moment your mum isn't aware that you visit the café for your in-between meals." She chuckled, when he looked surprised. "Your mum's no fool."

"Aye, I know that. Mum's brilliant." He rubbed at his head and then his belly. "I thought I'd hid my trips to the café from her."

"Deirdre is family, Niall. She was always going to tell Mary how you drop by every day around three." Smiling, Hettie shrugged. "You should have a kitchen installed in the saloon. That way the men could eat and drink." She smirked at him. "And you'd always have food available."

He groaned and shook his head. "It's enough work getting them all the whiskey they can drink. I don't have time for anything more." He gave a quick nod of his head toward his brother, Lucien. "Besides, Luc's too busy with Sammie and Etienne. We don't want to take on anything more."

Hettie smiled, as Winnie joined them. Slinging an arm over her best friend's shoulder, Hettie giggled, while she watched Winnie's three-year-old daughter chortle at something A.J. had said to her. The river captain and his wife, Bessie, had settled here the year Hettie had joined Winnie on her return to Fort Benton four years ago. Hettie laughed. "Ava's got A.J. wrapped around her finger."

"She does," Winnie said, with a soft smile. "Almost as much as she does her papa." Her smile deepened, when she looked toward her husband, Finn. Like many of the O'Rourkes, he was tall, with broad shoulders. His black hair was shaggy and in need of a cut, and his blue eyes sparkled with mischief, as he murmured something to his brother and best friend, Eamon. Together, they ran the successful family store.

Niall watched Hettie wander away to speak with his mum and youngest sister, Maggie, sighing with happiness that everyone he loved was in one place tonight. Nothing would ruin the joy he felt right now.

Hettie smiled and gave Maggie a quick hug, before lifting Maggie's two-year-old son, Lorcan, into her arms. She made faces at him, as he chattered away at her, before resting his head on her shoulder with a contented sigh. "Oh, he's a beautiful boy, Maggie."

Maggie watched her son with Hettie and smiled with pleasure. "Aye, he is. Dunmore's delighted, although he misses the days I traveled around the Territory with him. There weren't nearly enough of them."

"You mean, enough to satisfy his need to have you near," Hettie teased, as she watched the loyal stagecoach driver cast quick glances in their direction. Dunmore and Maggie had been married for nearly five years, and they still acted like newlyweds. Hettie dreamed of a marriage like theirs—or of any of the O'Rourke couples—but knew it was unlikely.

After passing Lorcan back to Maggie, Hettie moved around the chattering O'Rourkes, stilling when she heard Niall laughing and talking with his brothers Declan and Lucien. She heard Lucien teasing Niall and froze.

"You're the next to marry. It's not like you'll meet anyone better, Niall. She's good enough."

Had Niall met someone? Her mind raced at the thought. They were best friends, and she thought he'd tell her if he had. Although she hadn't told him about the man she'd met, so she supposed that was fair.

Not wanting to examine why she'd failed to tell Niall about Jacob, she smiled at Seamus and tried to act like she wasn't avidly listening in on the conversation occurring between the three brothers.

"*Good enough?*" Declan snorted. "Good enough for what? Why should he settle?"

"She's a good woman!" Niall protested.

"Aye, and your best friend, besides Luc," Declan muttered, humor in his voice. "But you deserve more, Niall." Declan grunted at the jab Niall landed to his shoulder and then laughed. "You know we all adore her, but if you don't ..."

Declan's voice faded away, as they were jostled into a corner and away from Hettie. Her breath ratcheted in and out of her, once she realized they were talking about her. That Declan thought Niall could do better than her. That Niall deserved *more* than a woman like her.

Paling, she realized the O'Rourkes really only saw her as the hired help. She was not part of this family, no matter what Niall proclaimed or how they acted. She would never be good enough.

Tamping down any foolish hopes, she pasted on a smile and focused on the fact that she did have a suitor. She would not be alone for long, if she didn't choose to be. The only problem was, she wouldn't be with the man she'd dreamed of for the last four years. Reminding herself how she was used to disappointment, she also scolded herself for feeling the sting of this heartache.

CHAPTER 2

Finally the congratulations and blessings had been bestowed on Bryan, and they trooped out of the house to the café. Niall was at her side again, eager to walk with her to the café for their supper and continued celebration for Bryan. "Did Deirdre already leave?" Niall asked.

Hettie laughed and nodded her head, although her friendliness seemed a little stilted.

What had happened since she had left his side in the kitchen? Niall wanted to pepper her with questions but bit his tongue.

She spoke, interrupting his thoughts. "Yes, along with Maggie, Niamh, and your mum. They wanted a supper prepared by the O'Rourke women."

"You're an O'Rourke woman," Niall objected, frowning as he saw her flush and shake her head. "You're one of us, Hett."

She frowned, staring at him a long moment, and he had a sudden worry that she thought he was mocking her. He hoped she saw nothing but sincerity in his gaze.

"You know I'm not, Niall. I'm Henrietta Foyle, with none who'd miss me if I died." When he gripped her arm and spun her, so she stopped her slow walk to the café's rear entrance, she gasped and shook her head in confusion. "Niall?"

"Don't say such foolish things, Hett. You know how much ... we'd all miss you." His green eyes glowed with unspoken and unacknowledged emotions, as he battled something he didn't understand. All he knew was that the conversation with his brothers had dredged up feelings he hadn't realized he had. Damn Declan for knowing just where to poke and to prod to get Niall all mixed up.

Shrugging, she ducked her gaze, her cheeks flushed. "Perhaps you would miss me, but I know who I am, Niall. An orphan." Her breath caught, as he stroked a finger over the soft skin of her cheek.

"Aye, you are. Just as my real mum's dead. But that doesn't mean I shut myself off from those who care about me, who cherish me." He shook his head, his gaze pinning her and keeping her immobile. "And don't spout any more nonsense about being the hired help."

At his disgruntled growl, she giggled. Her eyes glowed, and she shook her head. "I know you're thinking about our discussion."

"Discussion? That was a fight, Hett," he muttered, his green eyes shining with disgust. "I never want to hear you describing yourself as the hired help again to anyone, least of all to one of those drunks at the saloon. They won't understand how precious you are ..." His voice faded away, and he stared at her intently. "You can badger me all you want about that, but it's the truth."

A loud whistle carried on the gentle breeze, and they turned for the café. He knew this conversation was far from over, but he hated how she saw herself. He thought she understood that she was like a cousin to everyone and had only realized a week ago how deep her sense of insecurity ran.

Forcing a smile as he entered the café kitchen, he washed his hands and then helped move platters of food from the kitchen to the dining room, where smaller tables had been pushed together to form one huge table. Everyone, including Cormac and Dunmore, gathered here tonight. Married to Niamh and Maggie, the two men were usually busy ferrying freight and passengers throughout the Territory during the hectic summer months. However, they adored Bryan, as much as everyone else in the family, and had endeavored to be here.

Niall sat between Eamon on one side and Hettie on the other, while Niall waited for everyone to settle and for Da to say grace. Even though Niall was starving, he always enjoyed Da's short benedictions. They never failed to remind Niall to not take anything for granted and to always give thanks for everything he had.

"Today we express our gratitude for our continued successes, our health, this abundant meal, and our fine family. We're also particularly grateful for wee Bryan, who's growing into such a fine lad. For all this, we give our thanks."

At the chorus of "Amens," a multitude of hands reached forward to grab bowls and platters to pass around, as various conversations erupted. Niall listened to Eamon and Finn talk about customers they'd served that day, while Niall soaked up the joy of being surrounded by his entire family. He knew it would be unlikely to occur again until after the busy season was over, due to their many businesses and the need to keep them open so they remained profitable. It wasn't realistic to close the café and saloon for too many evenings during the short summer season, when the majority of the year they had few customers.

Turning his attention from his brothers, he focused in on Hettie's and Winnie's conversation, freezing when he realized what they discussed. "What?" he gasped. Looking down at Hettie, who was inches shorter than he was, whether standing or sitting, he tried to hide the sudden spurt of rage at what he thought he'd heard. "What did you say, Winnie?"

"It was nothing," Hettie blurted out, casting a warning glance at her friend.

However, either Winnifred didn't see it or chose to ignore it, as she smiled and blithely said, "Oh, Hettie has a suitor. Isn't that wonderful? After all this time, she has the chance to be as happy as I am!" Winnie sat on the other side of Hettie and leaned forward, ensuring Niall saw her delighted grin.

Swallowing a growl of rage, Niall attempted a smile but gave up that idea when Winnifred looked at him as though he were a petulant two-year-old. With a swift shake of his head, he focused on his full plate of food, but suddenly he wasn't hungry. The mashed potatoes, ham, and buttered peas were as unappetizing as any of the meals they'd scrounged together when he was a boy, before his da had success in business.

"I thought you'd be happy for me."

Hettie's soft words cut through him worse than any knife, and he nodded, staring blankly at his food. "Of course I am, Hett." Forcing himself to look at her, he smiled, although his gaze remained bleak. "Is he a good man?"

She blushed and gave a little excited squirm, increasing Niall's agony even more. Why? Why was her happiness killing him? He forced himself to focus on her, rather than on the devastation he felt, and waited for her to speak. When she remained quiet, he murmured, "His job, Hett. What's he do? How will he provide for you?"

When a boot rammed into his shin, he jerked and glared at his eldest brother, Ardan, seated across the table from him.

Ardan stated, "If Hettie likes him, we'll have him over for supper and make sure he's a nice man."

Niall nodded. Ardan's word was almost as hallowed as that of Da's. Besides, Niall wanted a chance to meet this ... man, this ... He shook his head, unable to come up with a word to describe the unknown man who had turned Niall's world upside down.

He sat in stilted silence, as he swallowed bite after bite of food that he no longer tasted, while he listened to Hettie talk and gush with Winnie about the man called Jacob. Why would she want him?

When Ardan tapped his leg gently this time, Niall looked up and saw that it was time to clear the table and to bring out Bryan's birthday cake. Forcing a joviality he no longer felt, Niall pasted on a smile and laughed at Henri's and Oran's antics, thankful that they were distracting him.

After piling the sink high with dishes, Niall returned to the dining room, stutter-stepping as a deep joy filled him at the delight and wonder in Bryan's expression. Niall suddenly wished he were as innocent as Bryan again. That Niall's worst travail was to miss out on a Mr. Pickens story.

Instead the woman he lo—he shook his head at the thought of using that word. *Loved?* Casting a furtive glance in Hettie's direction, he frowned. Of course he loved her. She was his best friend, besides Lucien, and Niall would maim anyone who tried to hurt her.

But love her? Like the way his da loved his mum? Or his brothers their wives? Niall's hands shook as he wiped at his brow, and he was shocked to feel sweat on his fingers. He was too young to feel anything more. He was too young to be tied down. He was only twenty-two. Why did anything have to change?

Glaring at Ardan, who stared at him knowingly, Niall forcefully focused on Bryan, who sat near Da at the head of the table, waiting for the birthday cake. At the hush and then the lilting first words sung by Deirdre, they all joined in, singing lustily.

When the large cake was set in front of Bryan, he closed his eyes, with his lips moving in a silent wish, and then he beamed at his family. "Thank you!"

Seamus hugged him from the side, while Mary stood behind him and squeezed his shoulders. "Ah, lad, you know how proud we are of you and how much you are loved." Seamus motioned at the entire family, either seated or standing around Bryan. "You never have to look far for someone who cares."

Bryan smiled and bit his lip, before blurting out, "Can everyone speak after we've eaten cake?" He flushed at the roar of laughter, although none argued with him. Deirdre's cakes were delicious and were always quickly devoured by the O'Rourke clan.

Thankfully Deirdre had made a few cakes for the large gathering, and there was plenty of chocolate and vanilla cake for those who wanted a second helping. Niall ate his slice of cake, savoring the sweet treat, as he considered what he wanted to do. Had he already lost Hettie to this other man?

When supper was over, the men insisted that the O'Rourke women leave the cleanup to them, as the women had already done enough planning and cooking of the huge family meal. First Niall ushered Mum home, puffing up with pride when he saw the approval in his da's gaze. When Niall returned, he moved to the café kitchen and started washing the dishes with Hettie, who offered to remain. Meanwhile Oran and Henri cleaned off the tables and moved them back to where they should go, before then sweeping the floors.

Now Niall was elbow deep in soapy water, trying to find a way to talk with Hettie, like he always had. Easy and lighthearted, like they didn't have a care in the world. Unfortunately he couldn't *act* around her. She always saw through him. Besides, she seemed preoccupied tonight.

"Tell me about him," he demanded, wincing, as the words emerged harsher than he intended. When he heard her sigh, he realized he'd gone about the entire situation wrong. He should have teased and cajoled and learned snippets of information from her and Winnie over time. Instead he'd stormed in, insisting she tell him everything.

Would she understand he was acting out of jealous spite? Or was that worse? Should he hope she'd think he was only protective and a little curious?

"Niall, there's little to tell you," she said in her softly accented voice that still held a hint of her native England. "I met a man who interests me and seems to like me too. I'll have to learn more about him, although I wonder if he'll be in town long enough to truly discern his character."

Niall paused and studied her false attempt at disinterest. "You were gushin' away tonight, as you chattered with Winnie, Hett. Don't think to say now that you aren't interested in the man." When she gaped up at him in confusion, he flushed. "Why won't you tell me about him?"

She fisted the damp dishtowel in her hands and shrugged. "Why should I have to? We're friends, Niall, but I don't owe you … You're not my …" Her eyes rounded, and her breath emerged quickly, almost in pants. "I shouldn't have said anything."

"I'm not what, Hett?" he asked in a low whisper, lowering his head, as he attempted to look into her eyes. "I'm nothin' more than your friend?"

When she jerked her head and spun away before he could catch her, he swore under his breath, watching as she raced away. "Hett!" he yelled after her, hating that she'd walk home alone. Marching to the back door of the café's kitchen, he descended the few steps, his gaze following her form, until he had confirmed that she'd returned to the big O'Rourke home safely.

Only then did he kick a rock and let out a soft roar, hopeful he wouldn't wake Ardan's son, Rory, sleeping above the café in their personal living quarters. Niall wished he could fight someone, especially this nameless Jacob person. Most of all, Niall wished someone would have bashed some sense into him *before* he was on the verge of losing the person he most cherished.

~

Hettie raced through the big O'Rourke house and up the stairs to her bedroom, ignoring Mary's call to join her for a cup of tea, shutting the bedroom door behind her. Thankfully Mary and Seamus understood that their children needed safe havens and places for contemplation away from the bustling family, and they rarely interrupted any of their children or adopted family members when bedroom doors were closed.

Grateful for a few small mercies, Hettie collapsed onto her bed and buried her face in her pillow, so the sound of her sobbing wouldn't carry. She'd hoped Niall would be pleased for her. Just as she would have attempted to be happy for him, if he'd found someone.

Instead he was acting like a petulant child, and she was sorely disappointed. She knew he didn't truly want her or love her. If he had, he would have done something in the past four years to proclaim himself. Instead he'd been perfectly content with their friendship.

Now, after the way his brothers had spoken tonight, she knew he was only acting interested in her because he'd yet to meet someone better in their small, isolated town in Montana Territory. Even Declan, who'd always been so kind and charming, thought Niall shouldn't settle for her.

Sighing, Hettie curled onto her side, admitting to herself that she'd been happy too over these four years, for the most part. As long as she ignored the incessant yearning for more. As long as she pushed aside the daydreams about him as a husband and father. As long as she saw the happiness of the many O'Rourke couples around her, knowing it would never be hers, she was able to delude herself that she was fulfilled with the life she led.

After living life as an orphan for too long and having no one care about whether she lived or died, she'd been shocked to receive the love and friendship from the O'Rourkes. She still considered herself the hired help, even though they ensured she had everything she needed to thrive, including a place to live, food, and clothes. More important, they'd showered her with love, friendship, and support.

Even though they treated her well, Hettie never failed to remind herself who she was. She was a woman hired to cook and clean and care for the children as needed. She was not family. She was not a woman who would marry into the family. Surely Seamus and Mary wanted a better woman for their sons than an orphan who'd begged and stolen to survive. Clearly his brothers were astute enough to know that.

Now Niall was stealing her chance to find happiness by acting like a spoiled child, and she didn't know how she'd forgive him. Hettie now knew she'd be denied a life with him, and she didn't want to live her life alone. If he were a true friend, he'd be happy for her.

Clinging to her righteous anger, so she wouldn't have to focus on the hurt underneath, Hettie curled even tighter onto her side. Tears continued to leak from her eyes, and she wondered if the pain and disappointment would ever ease. Would attempting a relationship with a man she could never love as she loved Niall be fair to anyone? Closing her eyes, she prayed for the oblivion of sleep, wishing everything would be different when she woke in the morning.

CHAPTER 3

The following day Niall wiped down the long counter at the saloon, just before opening time. He worked long hours during the busy season, as did all O'Rourkes. However, Niall tried to work extra, so his brother Lucien had time at home with his wife, Samantha, and son, Etienne. During the summer busy season, Niall rarely made it to his parents' house for supper, but he ensured his brother Lucien almost always made it home for dinner and bedtime with Etienne. Afterward, Lucien returned for the busy late-evening hours, when the saloon was packed with customers.

As the town grew, Niall knew they'd need more help in the saloon, and he wondered who his da would trust. Although he and Lucien ran it, it wasn't theirs alone but one of the many O'Rourke family businesses. Along with the saloon, the family owned the most profitable store in town, run by Finn and Eamon. Ardan and Deirdre ran the café, and Declan and Lorena a bookshop and a small school. The family also had a warehouse, run by Kevin and Oran, where they stored supplies for their numerous businesses.

As their families had grown, they'd devised a way to accommodate the children, so everyone could continue working. Most of the women of the family took turns, as they ran a sort of day care for all of the youngest O'Rourkes, and Niall sometimes wished he could skip the saloon to hang out with the little tykes. However, he was needed at the saloon, and he'd always do what his family needed him to do.

Glancing around the establishment, Niall noted how different it was now compared to four years, when they'd taken over the running of the saloon from Bell—who had been banished from Fort Benton and never seen again—presumed dead. Maggie's husband, Dunmore, who was the most successful stagecoach driver out of Fort Benton and heard the best gossip in the Territory during his travels, had told them in hushed conversations how he'd never heard any further word of Bell. Thus they all hoped Bell truly was out of their lives forever. Bell's former business partner, Uriah Chaffee, was rumored to be somewhere in the Territory, but he'd yet to return to Fort Benton.

As for the saloon, Seamus had remodeled it, proclaiming it might be a saloon, but it didn't have to appear like a den of iniquity. The poorly lit poker tables in the back had been removed, and now all parts of the saloon were well lit, with candelabras hanging over many of the tables. The long bar with the huge mirror behind it now shone with polish, rather than sweat or chewing tobacco, and the walls had been scrubbed clean of years' worth of tobacco smoke, until the pine shone again. Washing the windows regularly ensured bright light shone in, and the front door was almost always open during business hours, unless a torrential storm threatened outside.

Seamus had made one other major change in the running of the saloon. The serving women, called Temptresses, were gone. They had been offered work helping Ardan serve meals at the café or washing dishes and glasses at the saloon or café. Only one, Theresa, had opted to continue to work with the O'Rourkes, helping with a variety of jobs, from caring for the children to helping out at the saloon behind the scenes to serving patrons. A few of the Temptresses had opted to work at the Bordello, while the rest had scattered in the Territory.

"Where's Theresa?" Niall asked Lucien, who had strolled in a few minutes ago.

"Today's her day to watch the children."

Swearing under his breath, Niall sighed, as that meant they'd be shorthanded today. "Damn." He slammed a chair into place, gripping the wood like he wanted to rip it apart.

"What did the chair do to you?" Lucien asked, an amused glint in his hazel eyes.

"I'm bad company, Luc," he muttered, rubbing at his forehead. He'd barely slept all night, as his mind tormented him with images of Hettie and another man. Kissing him. Letting him hold her. And so much more. Swearing under his breath again, Niall marched to the back of the saloon, his heels clattering on the cellar steps, as he descended to check on the whiskey stores.

He had no reason to be down here, but he couldn't handle his brother's questions. Lucien knew him too well. Although they'd not been raised together, after Mary had returned to them eight years ago, they had become best friends. With a quick glance around the cellar, he knew that the whiskey stores were fine and that there was plenty of room for the next shipment, due any day.

Sighing, he sat on a crate, resting his elbows on his knees, wishing things were different. Now that Hettie had found someone else, Niall shouldn't ruin things for her. He should be happy for her.

Instead he wanted to rage and scream and ... He closed his eyes to calm his violent thoughts. He'd never thought himself capable of anything so brutal as murder, but now he wondered.

And why was he saying she'd found someone else? *Hettie and I have never been more than friends.* He'd loved her like he loved his sisters. Or sisters-in-law.

Liar, he whispered to himself.

Hettie had always been different to him. Special in a way he couldn't name, and he'd never wanted to examine why. There'd been no reason for things to change.

Until last night.

Now everything was different, and she was interested in this man called Jacob. If they'd met here in the saloon, he wasn't worthy of Hettie. Swearing, Niall rose and started to pace in and out of the shadows in the cellar, as the only light was from a lantern by the stairs.

How was he such an idiot? How could he not know he loved her? Truly loved her? Not like a sister or a cousin but like the woman he wanted to marry and grow old with? *"Eejit,"* he muttered to himself.

"Aye, that you are," a man called out in a deep, melodious voice. "What are you doin' pacing down here? Luc will need your help upstairs soon."

Niall spun and faced his eldest brother, Ardan. "Ard, I … I needed a minute to myself." Ardan stood in the faint light, and Niall saw the compassion and understanding in Ardan's gaze, which nearly gutted him. "I'm fine."

"You're far from fine, lad. You're in for the fight of your life, and you must come to the belief that you are worthy of fightin' it."

Paling, Niall shook his head. "I don't know what you mean." Straightening his shoulders and fisting his hands, as though preparing for a blow, he watched Ardan slowly approach him. Niall frowned when he could no longer clearly discern his brother's expression.

"Aye, you do know well what I mean, but you're not willin' to face it yet," he said, the soft lilt of Ireland still in his voice. Ardan came to a stop only a few feet away from Niall, slowly raising his hand to squeeze his brother's shoulder. "Colleen hurt you as much as any of us."

Swallowing, Niall jerked his head in denial. "I don't—"

"Don't, lad," Ardan murmured, as he shook his head, cutting off Niall's lie. "Lie to yourself if you must but not to me. I saw what she was doing. I know what she was. And I'm sorry I couldn't do more to protect you." Squeezing Niall's shoulder again, Ardan spoke in a raspy voice. "Some older brother I was."

"You did what you could." Niall cleared his throat. "Mu—" He broke off and shook his head, as the woman who was his mum was Mary. She was all that was good and loving and devoted. She was all he'd ever dreamed of in a mum as a boy. Never his own mother. Never Colleen. "Colleen did her best."

"Aye, her best to inflict damage you never overcame." Bending forward, Ardan's blue eyes shone with passion. "Don't let her ruin what you can have, Niall."

"It's too late, Ard. I ... I've lost her."

Rolling his eyes, Ardan released him and spun to pace away. "The lass is interested in a man who shows her some affection and showers her with sweet words. She's had little of that in her life. Don't lose her because you're too afraid to try, Niall. You'll never forgive yourself."

Niall shrugged, desire and uncertainty battling inside him.

"Don't be like Cormac," Ardan murmured.

Hissing in a breath, Niall nodded. He understood his brother's warning. Cormac had loved their eldest sister, Niamh, but had lost her to his own brother, Connor. Only after Connor's death did Cormac finally fulfill his dream of marrying and building a life with their eldest sister. "I'll try not to be."

Ardan swore in Gaelic and huffed out a breath. "Do more than *try*." He looked over his shoulder at Niall, nodded as though it were an order rather than a suggestion, and left.

Collapsing onto his crate again, Niall sat in a daze. He knew he should head upstairs to help Lucien, as the saloon was open, and they'd be busy. They were busy from the moment they opened until the second they pushed out the last customer each night.

Instead Niall remained seated, his mind conjuring memories of when he was a boy. He'd adored his da. Strong and loving and capable, Seamus had never run out of love for any of them. Whenever they had a problem or needed a hug or advice, he'd been their rock. The only one Da had never had an abundance of love for was his second wife, Niall's mother, Colleen.

Increasingly bitter, Colleen resented never being loved by Seamus. She had seen the way his children talked about their lost mum with a reverence and devotion, plus the look of longing in her husband's eyes, and a bitterness had bloomed in Colleen that her husband would never feel a fraction for her what he'd felt for the woman he'd lost. Colleen resented the easy love that passed between her husband and his children—not the stilted attempt at affection that she received from Seamus. Colleen's jealousy soured any chance she had at celebrating her own children's close relationship with their father, and she lashed out in every way she knew how.

Niall let out a shuddering breath, as he heard the echo of her words and her vicious cackle, especially when she saw how much her chosen words hurt Niall, tainting his childhood. Even though she had died years ago, Niall still fought those memories. Shaking his head, he rose, determined to put her taunts and curses behind him. He had to face the day and to find Hettie. He had to make her see that she didn't belong with anyone but him.

~

Hettie wandered around the saloon, clearing tables, before she hefted a heavy basket of linens to carry upstairs. Just as the downstairs had been remodeled, the upstairs had been equally transformed. Now four good-size rooms were rented out each night, and a few men had rented them for weeks at a time, as they got their bearings, before heading deeper into the Territory.

Seamus had insisted that the space would bear no resemblance to the tiny rooms, or cribs, that the Temptresses had used when Bell had owned the saloon. Now the rooms were spacious, with windows, and a small sitting area sat at the top of the stairs, so the guests could relax in a space away from the saloon, if they wanted.

Hettie helped as much as she could, doing every kind of job possible for the O'Rourkes. She watched the children, helped at the café and here at the saloon. Every day was different, and she loved it. If she were honest with herself, her favorite days were the ones she spent here because she was able to see Niall more.

Pushing him out of her mind, she focused on Jacob. He was smart and handsome and interested in her in ways Niall never would be.

Huffing out a pent-up breath, Hettie yanked out a sheet and flapped it open so hard it almost whacked her in the face. If she heard one more person say that she and Niall were like brother and sister, she'd scream. They weren't related. They never had been. And, with the way things were going, they never would be.

Fool that she was, she'd had a vague hope—when they first became close four years ago—that their friendship would develop into something more. It never had, and this past winter she'd resolved that she would not pine over Niall any longer. She'd not waste another season yearning for him. She'd find a man who actually wanted more from her.

A broken heart and disappointed dreams notwithstanding.

Looking up at the noise at the door, she smiled at Winnie, as she bustled into the room. "Where's Ava?" Hettie asked.

"Oh, Theresa's watching her," Winnie murmured, as she grabbed the other side of the sheets and ably made the bed with Hettie. "Ava loves playing with Theresa and didn't cry when I left."

Smiling, Hettie nodded. "Few of the O'Rourke children cry when their parents leave, though I suspect it's because they're all together, playing like a pack of heathens." She winked at Winnie, as that was their running joke: that the next generation of O'Rourkes would be heathens, hell-bent on causing mischief in the Territory. Seamus was determined they'd leave their mark on this land and be more than shopkeepers and bartenders.

"Ah, little heathens, that they are," Winnie said, with an impish smile, "and now you have a chance to join our group. Perhaps you'll have your own child soon." She wriggled her eyebrows at her friend, as Hettie swatted a pillowcase at her and admonished her to hush. "Tell me more about this Jacob. It was hard to focus last night, with everyone chattering all around us and Niall acting worse than Ava."

"What do you mean?" Hettie perked up at the mention of Niall, although she tried to dampen her reaction to him. She feared she'd have the same response upon hearing his name even when she was ninety.

Winnie paused and fixed her friend with an exasperated stare. "Surely you saw how overprotective he became at the mere mention of the man? Just like any of the lads when one of their toys is taken away." Winnie sighed and slapped a hand onto one hip. "I don't know why he's surprised you'd look for romance during the busy summer season."

Swallowing, Hettie turned away to hide her suddenly crimson cheeks. "I wondered why he was so annoyed with me."

"You know men, Hettie." Winnie led the way out of the room, as they moved to the next bedroom to change the sheets. "He doesn't like change, and you meeting and falling in love with someone new is definitely change. So tell me about this man."

Shrugging, Hettie smiled and stared into space a minute. "It's like I said last night, Winnie. I've only spoken to him a few times, when I work at the café. And I've seen him around town twice. He's always polite, and he's asked me out to supper, but I'd hate to go to the other café."

Winnie made a gagging sound, as the other café had a horrible reputation. "You could go on a picnic."

Shaking her head, Hettie smiled at her friend. "No, I'd want to know him more before I did that. I'm in no rush to do anything rash."

"Well, the season's short, so I wouldn't take too long deciding if you like this Jacob. If you don't like him, other men will come through town."

Hettie smiled, although she wondered if any man would match her feelings for Niall. Letting out an aggrieved huff, she was determined that it didn't matter. No matter what, she'd find a way to like Jacob enough. She had to. She wanted a husband and children and her own home. She wanted what Winnie had with Finn.

One way or another, Hettie would find a way to have it.

An hour later, after all the beds had clean linens, the rooms were tidied,, and the common area spotless, Hettie descended the stairs. She skirted the tables and moved to the back room to deposit her cleaning bucket and to wash up, before heading to the café. Usually she'd wait for Niall to sneak in and chat with her for a few minutes, but today she wasn't in the mood to speak with him.

Leaving out the back door, she wandered in the direction of the nearby café, turning her head up to the bright sun. Knowing she shouldn't linger outside or risk getting burned, she still meandered off course to walk near the small creek that fed the Missouri River.

Niall had introduced her to the spot, telling her that the O'Rourkes came here to think and to have important discussions. Taking a deep breath, Hettie focused on the melodious trickle of the water over the rocks, ignoring the nearby sounds of men hollering, hammers slamming into wood, and wagons coming and going. They were all sounds she was used to and accustomed to drowning out.

The only sound she truly hated was gunfire. Too many of the itinerant men liked to shoot at things in the middle of the night, when they were drunk and wanted a shooting match, before going back to drink some more. She spent too many evenings and early mornings listening to them, before tumbling into sleep for a few hours, then starting another long day of work.

What she wouldn't give for the quiet and peace of the slow season, all year-round.

She heard footsteps behind her and turned her head, expecting to see Niall or another O'Rourke. Instead she saw Jacob Morrissey. "Sir!" she gasped, spinning to face him.

"I don't mean to frighten you, miss." He paused a few paces away from her and doffed his hat, raising a hand to ruffle his blond hair, after it had been squashed by his hat. He squinted at her in the bright sunlight, his long fingers playing over the brim of his hat, as though battling nerves. He stood with his shoulders back, as tall as any of the tallest O'Rourke men. "I've been hoping to see you."

Staring at him in confused silence for a moment, Hettie finally blurted out, "Why?"

He took a hesitant step in her direction and then paused. "Because I'm to leave town in about one week's time. I'm hoping to know you better before I do."

Frowning, Hettie raised a hand to shield her eyes from the sun and to see him better. "Why?" she asked again, thoroughly confused. When he took the last step that separated them and grasped her hand, she gasped.

"Because I'm hoping you'll learn enough about me by then to agree to travel with me into the Territory. To become my wife."

Her eyes bulged, and she gaped at him. "Mr. Morrissey!" Holding her free hand to her chest, she struggled to find something to say. "I, ... I ..."

He smiled at her, his blue eyes shining with sincerity. "I know I've taken you by surprise, but I've never been a man to let something or, in this case, someone, I want slip out of reach without a fight. I could tell from first meeting you that you are an upstanding woman. A woman who'd stand by my side and meet the challenges that will come from living in such a wild place."

When he stroked a finger over her silky-smooth check, he shocked her into silence. "No, Miss Foyle, there's no need to say anything. Merely promise me that you'll consider what I've said. And agree to dine with me this week?"

"Yes," she murmured. "Perhaps more than once if you are serious."

He chuckled, a warm, soothing sound pleasant to Hettie's ears. "I'm very serious." His blue eyes were warm as he gazed at her. "Tomorrow night?"

Hettie nodded. "I'll meet you ..."

"No." He squeezed her hand. "I'll come to the O'Rourke house and walk you to supper, as any man worth his weight courting you should."

She flushed and nodded. "Until tomorrow night." Her flush deepened at the husky sound of her voice.

He gave a subtle bow and strode away, slipping his hat back on. Hettie watched his long, smooth strides and wondered what had just happened. Then, just as quickly, panic filled her at the prospect of leaving Fort Benton and the place that had been her home for four years. Of leaving the O'Rourkes. Could she bear it?

She pushed away thoughts of Niall, as contemplating leaving him and never seeing him again caused such a deep anguish that she wasn't sure she would survive. However, Niall wasn't offering her anything. Mr. Morrissey was. Only a fool turned down a certainty in the hopes of an elusive dream coming true someday.

CHAPTER 4

During a small lull in the afternoon business, Niall saw Lucien chatting with a customer at the other end of the bar. As that conversation ended, Lucien sauntered in his direction, smiling and calling out greetings to everyone present. They treated their customers more like friends or guests than paying customers, and the atmosphere was more convivial than other saloons in town.

Lucien picked up a glass and acted like he was swiping it dry, as he spoke softly to his brother. "What's the matter with you? You're glowering at everyone."

"I need to get away for a little while. Can you cover me?"

Lucien looked around the room, before he nodded.

Heaving out a breath of relief, Niall thumped Lucien's back and slipped out from behind the bar and then out the back door. When he got outside, he paused for a moment, blinded by the brilliant sunlight.

In the distance, he saw Henri and Bryan heading out on an adventure, and he called out for them. After they'd raced in his direction, he couldn't help but smile. How were they only four years younger than him? He felt ancient compared to them, with their youthful exuberance and naive hopefulness shining in their gazes. "Can you go to the saloon? Help Luc?"

Bryan gasped with delight. "Da said I wasn't allowed there."

"Aye, until you were a man. You are now." Niall winked at him, as Bryan puffed out his chest and crowed with delight, racing in the direction of the saloon. Watching them nearly rip the door off the back of the saloon in their exuberance, Niall hoped he hadn't made a terrible decision. However, Luc and he needed help at the saloon, and the lads were old enough to work there. He and Lucien had taken over the running of it when they were barely older than Henri and Bryan were now.

Turning for the café, Niall put thoughts of his youngest brothers out of his mind and focused on what he had to do. On what he hoped to say. His confident steps faltered, when he had no idea what he would say.

His mind spun at the thought of blurting out how he loved her, but that's what he wanted to do. Would she believe him?

Taking a deep breath, he strolled into the café and froze at the sight of Hettie laughing at the story Deirdre was telling her. Her head was tipped back, her golden hair was in a loose braid down her back, soft wisps framing her face, and her eyes sparkled with joy. She'd never looked more beautiful. "Hettie," he whispered.

She spun, her eyes widening, and a gasp of distress sputtered out.

Why would his presence bother her? Stepping forward to soothe her, he froze when he saw her jerk away from him. Why was she afraid of him? "Hettie?"

"Niall," she said in a flat tone, one he'd never heard before in her softly accented voice. "I thought you were busy at the saloon."

"There's a lull, and I thought you might like to take a walk. If you're not too busy." He looked around the kitchen and saw that it was mostly tidy. Few dishes needed washing, and the prep for the supper rush had been started. He watched as she and Deirdre exchanged a quick look and wished he'd mastered the art of deciphering that secret language women shared. Somehow he'd never picked it up from his eldest sister, Niamh, when he was a boy.

He stiffened when Hettie let out an aggrieved huff and jerked off her apron. He was quick to add, "You don't have to. I thought you'd want to get outside and to enjoy a bit of fresh air." He frowned when she gave him an exasperated look and then marched past him.

When Deirdre murmured, "Tread carefully," he nodded his head and followed Hettie outside, their usual carefree camaraderie missing. "Hett? What did I do?"

She strode ahead of him, ignoring his question. Just as they were about to reach the creek, he grabbed her arm and spun her to face him. "Dammit, Hett, what's the matter?" He blanched at the mixture of anger, hurt, and disappointment he saw in her gaze.

"Why are you here today, Niall? Why now?"

"If I can, I always come 'round to see if you want to go out for a walk." He frowned. "Why should it be any different today?" Seeing how upset she was, he quickly decided now would not be the ideal time to confess how much he cared for her.

She squirmed under his light hold of her arm, so he released her. She turned to face away from him, hiding any chance he had of seeing her emotions. He'd never had to guess what she felt in the past, and he hated this sensation of not knowing what bothered her and why. "Did someone hurt you, Hett?"

He shuffled around her, so he was in front of her, and bent low, so he was at her eye level. His green eyes shone with anger at the thought of anyone harming his precious Hettie. "If that bastard who's been talkin' with you hurt you in any way ..." He broke off what he would say when she laughed and rolled her eyes.

"Why would you think *he* was the one who hurt me, Niall?" she asked in a soft voice, laced with a devastating pain.

"Who else? I heard last night about him sniffing around, and today you're prickly and in a foul mood." He bit off what more he would have said when she flushed and looked like she was on the verge of heaving him into the small creek.

"So the only reason you care is because I've finally attracted the attention of a viable suitor?" She lifted her brows and waited for him to speak, nodding with indulgent pity when he sputtered out incomprehensible sounds. "Or is it because you think I'm too naive and stupid to discern a good man from a bad one?"

She waited, but by this point, Niall had wisely learned to bite his tongue, and he merely stared at her.

"Or is it because you're such an awful friend that you can't be happy for me and my good fortune?" She poked him in his chest, earning a yowl of pain as he backed up a step.

"Hett! We know nothing about him. Who are his people? Will he treat you well?" He paused, as he swallowed and whispered, "Will he take you away from us?"

Squaring her shoulders, Hettie lifted her chin and met his gaze. "I will decide those questions for myself. I'm a woman alone in this world and—" She squealed when he gripped her by the waist and tugged her closer to him.

"You sure as hell are not," he growled, forgetting his promise to himself not to swear around her. She was making him mad with envy and fear. "You've all the O'Rourkes, eager to look out for you. Don't forget that, Hett."

His gaze bore into hers, and, for one wild minute, he was tempted to kiss her and to show her just how much he loved her. As he bent his head, his breath fanning over her cheeks, he saw tears glistening in her eyes, and he swallowed, silently cursing himself to hell for ever causing her pain.

Releasing her, he stepped to the side, heaving out a deep breath. "Hett, I'm sorry."

"Just let me go, Niall," she whispered, ducking her head and racing away from him.

He watched her, murmuring, "I'll never let you go." Somehow he had to find a way to make her understand everything had changed between them.

～

Later, after an exhausting day helping Deirdre in the café kitchen, Hettie rushed from the café to the big O'Rourke house, determined to have supper with the family tonight. She missed a lot of family suppers during the busy season, but she liked to make the ones she could. She dodged men who loitered in the street behind the businesses, coming to a halt when a woman stepped in front of her path. "If you'd excuse me."

"Oh, aren't you a fancy one," snarled the older woman in worn clothes. "You think you're high and mighty because you're affiliated with the O'Rourkes, don't you?"

Hettie paused, her attempts at sidestepping the woman having failed. After a long moment, she squinted and then backed up a pace. "I know who you are. You're Mrs. Davies, and I've nothing to say to you."

This was Aileen O'Rourke's horrible aunt, the woman who had raised Aileen and had abused her confidence and nearly had convinced her to marry the wrong man. Instead Aileen had married Kevin, and they were happy. Hettie suspected they were most content because Janet Davies had been barred from having anything to do with the O'Rourke family.

The older woman gripped Hettie's arm, earning a hiss of pain. "Good, because I've plenty to say to you. You think you're so special? You're nothing. You might have a man interested in you right now, but he'll see you're nothing more than a poor servant girl, and he'll come to his senses." She cackled. "Why do you think that O'Rourke boy never wanted anything to do with you? Why settle for the hired help, when he could find someone better?"

Hettie flinched, her determination to ignore the bitter old woman's words failing. She felt like she'd just been sucker punched. Or at least she imagined this was how that felt. Gasping for breath, she wrenched her arm loose and glared at Mrs. Davies. "You have no right to speak to me like this."

"Oh, are you upset because I dared to speak the truth? Or is it

31

because he only cares about you now that he might lose you? A man like that is too fickle to ever be constant in his affection."

Hettie rushed away from her, flinching at the malicious cackling she heard behind her. Why had she had the misfortune to run into her today? Now her evening was ruined, as her mind spun with even more doubts and worries.

How did Janet Davies know about Jacob's interest in her? And why was she tormenting her about Niall? Scurrying around the side of a building, she leaned against it in the shadows, attempting to calm herself as she battled tears. If even Janet Davies, a woman who'd been relegated to the periphery of life in Fort Benton, knew that Niall would never consider Hettie good enough, then Hettie really was a hopeless dreamer.

Why had she been such a fool to imagine a life with him all these years? Why hadn't she accepted what she'd been shown to be true at a younger age? That she was unwanted and not worthy of loving?

She let out a deep breath and forced herself to relax, taking comfort in the fact that at least Niall wouldn't be home for supper tonight. She wouldn't have to see him again today. If she were lucky, she wouldn't have to face him until she'd made her decision.

Declan slipped into the saloon, nodding to Lucien, who worked the side of the long wooden bar nearest the front door. Strolling into the room, chatting with the men at the tables, Declan made his way to the far end of the bar, so he could sit near Niall. He leaned casually against the bar, with one hip resting against it, appearing as though he had no care in the world.

Nodding his thanks as Niall set a fingerful of whiskey in front of him, Declan turned so both elbows were on the bar, and he focused fully on his younger brother. "What's gotten into you?" Declan asked in his softly accented voice. "I hear you've tried to start three brawls today."

"They had it comin'," Niall snapped, tilting his jaw up and glaring at the men who'd approached them.

Although they most likely wanted a drink, Declan suspected they also wanted a portion of gossip, and he had no desire for them to linger nearby. "You know the rules, Niall. Smile and act nice and take their coin. They've done nothin' to you." His blue eyes shone with sincerity. "Da will be angry when he hears."

Niall slammed down a glass he'd been polishing for no good reason and leaned forward to whisper at his brother. "Why didn't you show me what a fool I was before last night? Why'd you wait until it was too late?"

Declan frowned and shook his head. "What do you mean?" When he saw the misery in Niall's expression, Declan chortled and slapped his hand on the bar. "Oh, *Jaysus*, you've finally figured it out?"

"'Tisn't funny, Dec!" Niall snapped.

Declan motioned for him to follow him into the back room, leaving Lucien to run the saloon, with the help of Bryan and Henri. When Declan shut the door to the small sink area, he crossed his arms over his chest and studied Niall. "You should be happy you've finally realized how much you care for Hettie. It's about time you stopped circling around her. She's a fine woman, and someone will come along and steal her from you, if you're not careful."

Niall glared at him, punching him in his arm for good measure. "That's the problem, Dec. Someone already has." When Declan gaped at him, Niall nodded and then rubbed his head, moaning in agony. "Hett thinks I'm acting like a spoiled brat, worried my favorite toy is being stolen away from me. She can't or won't believe I really care for her."

"*Love* her," Declan said in a soft voice, his blue eyes shining with compassion, as he waited for Niall to disagree with him. When his brother seemed to crumple in front of him, Declan swore softly and pulled Niall close. "I only meant to give you a push by saying all that garbage last night about doing better. Hettie's the best woman you could ever love."

Niall clung to his brother for a moment, before pushing away. "I know. But she doesn't want me. She doesn't believe me." He shrugged. "She thinks she can do better."

Declan gripped his shoulder and waited until Niall met his gaze. "Bull. Convince her how wrong she is. Don't live a lifetime of regret, Niall. You deserve better than that." He waited, hoping to hear Niall agree. When he remained silent, Dec murmured, "So does she. Never doubt it. For there is no better man in the world for her than you."

Declan squeezed Niall's shoulder one more time, before releasing him and slipping out the back door, understanding Niall needed to work. Declan only hoped Niall would be able to convince Hettie of his sincerity soon. Declan hated seeing his brother in so much pain.

CHAPTER 5

The following evening Hettie ran a hand over her burgundy skirt and patted at her hair. She wore a long-sleeved cream-colored shirt that buttoned at her wrists, as small bruises were forming where Mrs. Davies had grabbed her. Hettie preferred to avoid any questions tonight.

Staring at herself in the mirror, she sighed in defeat. She wished she had Winnie's natural exuberance and beauty, but she didn't. She was quieter and more reserved, until she was comfortable with someone, and then she opened up and felt free to express who she was. Few men had ever had the patience to want to get to know her. Only Niall truly did.

"Look where that got me," she muttered to herself, before taking a deep breath and forcing away any thoughts of him.

She'd already lost enough sleep thinking about their conversation by the creek. It meant nothing. It could mean nothing. She tried to ignore what Mrs. Davies had said, but the truth in her words had poisoned Hettie's dreams even further, and she no longer knew what to believe.

Pacing her small room, she worried Mr. Morrissey had decided not to escort her to supper. Just as she was about to go downstairs to join the O'Rourkes for their family supper, a knock on her bedroom door interrupted her erratic movement around her small room. "Yes?"

"A man's come calling to take you out, Hettie," Bryan O'Rourke called out, before she heard his bootsteps racing away. With her luck, he was racing back to the saloon to tell Niall all about Jacob's arrival to escort her to dinner.

With another deep breath, Hettie calmed her nerves and then left her room. As she descended the stairs, she paused at the second-to-last riser, just before she would be visible, because she heard the soft, deep murmur of men talking.

Seamus was interrogating Mr. Morrissey.

With a shake of her head, she realized she shouldn't be surprised.

Descending the last two steps and turning into the front room, she pasted on a bright smile and faced the men, unable to hide her shock at Niall's presence too. "Mr. Morrissey," she murmured. "How nice to see you."

He strode to her, lifting her hand to his mouth for a quick kiss, as his blue eyes gleamed with happiness. "How lovely you look tonight, Miss Foyle." He held out his elbow. "If I might escort you to the café?" Glancing at Seamus and Niall, he grinned. "I've assured them that I'll take you straight there and back again. And your brother of sorts, Ardan, will be there to ensure I am a perfect gentleman while at the café."

"A sort of chaperone," Niall said in a soft voice, laced with a warning for Mr. Morrissey.

Hettie cast Niall a quick glare, before smiling at Jacob. "A sound plan. Should we go?" Remaining in this room with Niall glowering at her was unbearable. She wanted to scream at him that she'd done nothing wrong but knew it wasn't worth wasting her breath.

Jacob winked at her and led her out the rarely used front door and toward the busier Front Street that faced the levee and the river. "They seem a wonderful family and are quite protective of you."

Flushing, Hettie nodded. "They took me in when I arrived. I'm most fortunate." She waited for him to say more, but he merely made a noncommittal sound, as they slowly walked toward the café. Men loitered outside, talking loudly, arguing over who had the correct version of a tall tale, or bent over a crate, as they bet on dice or cards. They were whiling away their time as they waited their turn to head into the Territory on one of the stagecoaches.

"You said you'd secured your seat in about one week's time, Mr. Morrissey?" She looked up and saw that he'd been watching her.

"Please, call me Jacob." He waited until she gave a soft nod and then nodded himself. "Yes, I leave in a week. I could kick myself, but I didn't plan well. I only have one ticket."

She stopped abruptly, nearly pulling free her hand looped through his arm. "I beg your pardon. I must have misunderstood what you said by the creek." She furrowed her brows, as she thought about that conversation. How could she have imagined he'd said he wanted to marry her and have her travel into the Territory when he hadn't?

"No. You didn't mishear or misunderstand anything, Henrietta." He stopped and faced her, wholly focused on her, his gaze sincere and his smile chagrin-filled. "Might I call you Henrietta?" At her nod, he gripped her hand and squeezed it. "I want everything I said to you by that creek. But I have to leave in a week. If you're brave and willing to take a chance on me, you'll have to travel to meet me alone."

"Alone?" Hettie whispered, as she looked around her at the men staring at her. She knew she had a measure of protection here in Fort Benton due to the O'Rourkes, but she feared that would end once she got on a stagecoach. "I don't know."

He ran a finger down her cheek and bent forward. "For now, let's have supper and chat. What happens in a week is something to worry about then, all right?"

She smiled at him and looped her hand through his arm again. "All right." She looked out at the beautiful cliffs across the river, gleaming gold in the early evening sun, and listened for the soft sound of the river, barely discernible under the town's racket.

Upon entering the café, Ardan seated them at a table by the window but in the corner, so they had privacy. She smiled her thanks at him and sighed with delight.

"I hope that was a good sigh," Jacob teased.

She blushed. "Yes. I rarely rest for meals in the busy summer season, and it's a treat to be here at the café and not in the kitchen." She paled and spoke hastily. "Not that I don't love working with Deirdre."

His smile was filled with kindness and a burgeoning affection, as he stared at her. "I'm certain she wishes she could have a night off here and there too. It seems like that family enjoys hard work."

Tilting her head to one side, Hettie asked, "Don't you?"

"Of course I do, but I'm fortunate that I have enough money now so I don't have to work all hours of the day anymore." He shrugged. "I'm here for the adventure."

Hettie frowned and shook her head. "That can't be the entire reason. There has to be more."

A shadow flickered across his face, and then he forced a smile. "Of course there is, and I'll tell you more later. For now, let's enjoy a good meal and a good conversation."

Hettie nodded and relaxed, focusing on learning everything she could about him, so she could discern if Jacob could expel Niall from her heart. Soon he was regaling her with tales of what had occurred in the past year, when Fort Benton had been isolated from the rest of the world. Fascinated by all he had to tell her, she forgot her worries and enjoyed his company.

With a sigh, Hettie shut the front door and leaned against it for a long moment. The entire evening had been enjoyable. After talking about recent events, they'd talked and laughed and shared crazy stories about their childhoods. He'd been born in England too, although he'd managed to drop his accent to better assimilate. She'd not learned what had caused the momentary glimpse of deep sorrow she'd witnessed, but she somehow knew he'd share it with her soon.

Although she'd only just met him, she sensed Jacob was a trust-worthy man. He was funny and attentive and kind. He was patient when she told rambling stories. He was protective, as when a drunk man approached, and he stepped in front of her and ensured the inebriated man left her alone. She'd been afraid for Jacob, as too many men carried guns and felt free to use them, but Jacob had shown no fear, only a determination that she be safe.

After the drunk man had stumbled away, Jacob had held her in his arms for a long moment, with her cheek pressed against his chest, where she heard his racing heart, belying his outward calm. Then he'd eased her away and quietly escorted her home. Although she would have considered kissing him, he had merely kissed her hand again and smiled at her.

"Until two evenings from now," he'd murmured, having secured the promise of another dinner with her.

Sighing, she was overwhelmed by his gallantry and the affection he showed her. But a stubborn piece of her heart screamed at her that it wasn't right for her to be out with him. It wasn't proper for her to have dinner with any man who wasn't Niall. Why did she feel so disloyal to a man who only saw her as his sister?

"Why the sigh, Hett?"

Gasping, she pushed away from the door and lurched into the darkened living room. "You waited up for me?" she hissed, as she glared at Niall. She couldn't make out his expression, but she saw the outline of his shoulders, and he was as tense as she'd ever seen him. "What's happened? Who's hurt?"

"What are you talkin' about, lass?" He took a step toward her, his face now lit by a shaft of light.

She blanched at the rage and agony in his beautiful green eyes. "Niall? What's wrong?"

"How was your dinner?"

She froze at his question, at the harsh rasp of his voice and the menacing undertone. "Fine." Shrugging, she attempted to act nonchalant, as she inched away from him. She couldn't remember seeing him this way before. Irate and hurt and itching for a fight. He'd never been like this with her before.

"Fine? That's all you have to say, when you've been gone for hours?" He took a huge step and was suddenly chest to chest to her. "You were only supposed to be out for supper."

"What are you, my brother?" She shook her head. "No. You're not, Niall. You're not anything. Not my brother. Not my father. Not my cousin. Nothing. You have no right to stand here and act like I did something wrong because I went out to dinner and enjoyed a conversation with a nice man."

"How'd you know he's nice?" He pounced on her comment, his eyes glowing with agony.

"From what I can tell, he is." She held up her hand. "And, no. You cannot interrogate him. You cannot accidentally run into him and have a thirty-minute conversation, where you scare him away." Her eyes shone with sincerity. "Leave me alone, as I determine if I like him enough to …"

Niall rocked back, as though she'd struck him. "To what, Hett?" When she remained quiet, he rasped, "To marry the man?" At her subtle nod of her head, he swore and paced away from her, his hand massaging the back of his neck. She knew him well enough to know he wanted to roar and scream, but that he wouldn't because it would wake the whole house and would bring too many O'Rourkes running and asking questions, which neither of them wanted to answer.

"I need my own life, Niall."

"Damn you, Hett," he rasped, spinning and marching toward her. "We have a life." Gripping her shoulders, he dragged her to him, his eyes wet and filled with despair. "We already have a life."

He ducked his head, and she braced for a bruising kiss. Instead he softly pressed his lips to hers, teasing her with his gentleness, his reverence evoking a sigh. With her sigh, he deepened the kiss, hauling her into his arms, his hands digging into her back and her hair, holding her so close; it was as though he'd never let her go.

They kissed and kissed, until they were breathless and shaking. Suddenly Hettie squirmed and pushed at him. "No!" She gasped and swiped at her mouth and moaned in distress. "No, Niall. No!"

Stumbling away from him, her legs tangled in her skirts, and she fell to her knees. "Let me go."

"Can't you see I can't, lass?" he whispered, falling to his knees to be beside her, his hands still touching her in any attempt to soothe her. "I *can't*, Hett. Ask anything of me but that."

"Why?" she cried out, tears coursing down her cheeks.

Kissing her head softly, he whispered, "Because I love you."

"No!" She pushed at him and crawled away, until she could press up and stand, holding a hand out and shaking her head, so he wouldn't approach her. "No, you don't get to say that to me now. Not now. Not when I have a chance with a man who, … who …" Tears coursed down her cheeks. "I'm not some toy, Niall. You don't get to play with me because you're afraid you'll lose me."

"Hett," he rasped, his voice like sandpaper. "It's not like that at all."

"It's exactly like that," she whispered, unable to speak any louder. "I never thought you so cruel." She spun on her heels, racing upstairs, desperate to get away from him.

She shut the door to her room, leaning against it as a sob escaped again. How could her glimmer of hope for a life with Jacob have been turned on its head in a matter of minutes?

Her fingers traced her lips, still tender from their kiss. Her scalp tingled where Niall's fingers had dug into the back of her head, as he held her in place to better kiss her. She felt branded and alive, and how dare he? How *dare* he tell her he loved her all because he was afraid she'd leave? All because he didn't like change?

Another sob escaped, and she swallowed it. If Mary heard her crying, she'd investigate, and Hettie feared Seamus would storm out of the house to inflict bodily damage on Jacob, when it was his own son who'd made Hettie cry.

Sliding down the door, until she rested on the floor, she wrapped her arms around her knees and yearned for simpler days. For those early days after she'd just arrived, and she was so thankful for friendship. When she wasn't looking for anything more. Instead she had heartache and confusion and misery as her bedfellows.

Would she ever be at peace again?

S torming into the saloon, Niall glared at Lucien to prevent him from asking any questions. He served customers, cleaned tables, swiped up messes, and listened to stories, all while his mind whirled.

She didn't want him. Hettie didn't want him.

After everything they'd done and been to each other, she didn't want him or his love. He gripped a glass so tightly, he feared it would shatter under his hold, and he set it down, his hand shaking. Clasping the hardwood of the bar, he leaned forward and lowered his head, as he fought a deep rage.

Oh, how he wished someone were looking for a fight. He'd gladly challenge that man tonight. But none were stupid enough to act out of line in Seamus O'Rourke's saloon. None wanted to be denied the opportunity of drinking the best whiskey in Fort Benton.

A coin slapped down on the bar in front of him, and he pushed back, tamping down his soul-deep despair. "What do you want?" He knew his da would skin him alive if he heard how surly he was talking to a customer.

"A little whiskey and a story."

Niall reared back and met the compassionate gaze of A.J. Pickens. Once one of the foremost riverboat captains on the Missouri, he'd settled in Fort Benton four years ago with his wife, Bessie. They'd left behind their life in Saint Louis, and Niall always wondered when they'd become restless and move on again. "Sir, I have whiskey but no story."

"Ah, so you believe," he said, his brown eyes gleaming with a keen understanding that seemed to home in on Niall's heartache, without having to ask any questions. "Your ladylove turned you down, and you're acting like a child."

He gaped at A.J. and shook his head in wonder. "How do you know that?"

Sipping at the whiskey in front of him, the older man—who was like an uncle to many of the O'Rourkes—shrugged. His wistful smile and the fond glint in his gaze eased Niall's annoyance at having been so obvious in his distress. "Oh, I was in your shoes once. I thought I'd lost the woman I loved. But I didn't." He grinned slyly at Niall and took another small sip, hissing as the burning liquid went down.

"How did you win her back?" Flushing at blurting out his question, Niall nevertheless leaned forward, desperate to know the answer. He'd do anything to win Hettie's affections.

A.J. leaned forward, his arms resting on the bar. "Well, I learned what she was so scared of and eased her of those fears. And proved to her that I wasn't a fickle man." He stared at Niall, with a hint of confusion in his gaze. "How in tarnation doesn't that girl already understand that about you?"

Niall pinched the bridge of his nose and closed his eyes for a moment, before meeting A.J.'s gaze. "She thinks I'm afraid of change and thinks I'm only claiming to like her, as more than a friend, so she won't leave." He looked at A.J. helplessly. "I don't know how to prove to her that I've always felt this way, but I was a silent *eejit* all those years."

"Aye, you're an idiot to talk about it here," Lucien muttered, as he approached with a warning glint in his gaze. "I've had to hustle a few men away from your area, so they won't listen in on your conversation."

"Why should they care about my problems?" Niall hissed, standing tall and glaring at the men in the saloon. Most weren't paying him any attention, but those who looked in his direction blanched and quickly averted their gazes. None sought out a fight with him. Although he wasn't tall like Ardan, he was burly and strong, and few wanted to start anything with him.

A.J. took one more sip of his whiskey, before setting it down and pushing away from the bar. He spoke in a soft voice that only Niall and Lucien could hear. "What I would say, lad, is to figure out what your lady needs to hear and see an' feel, then do whatever that is. Don't live with a lifetime of regret, sonny." He strolled away, calling out greetings to many of the men, causing everyone to laugh and to focus on him, rather than Niall.

"What's going on?" Lucien asked in a low voice.

"I'll tell you after we close." When Lucien nodded, Niall heaved out a sigh of relief that Lucien was willing to sacrifice a little of his time with Sammie so Lucien could support Niall. Focusing on his job again, Niall somehow got through the rest of the evening, until they closed the saloon down a little after one.

"Da wonders if we shouldn't stay open later," Lucien mused around a loud yawn. "I don't know how we'd manage."

"Even if Bryan and Henri worked here with us all the time, it would be a challenge," Niall said, as he cleared tables and brought dirty glasses to the small kitchen-like area, where they washed the glasses. "I'll come in early tomorrow and wash up everything."

"No," Lucien said, as he began washing dishes, "we'll do it now, and you'll tell me what's going on." His hazel eyes shone with curiosity and concern.

Lucien wasn't truly related to Niall by blood, as Mary was Lucien's mum with a French-Canadian trapper named Francois Bergeron for a father. However, Francois had died a year before Mary and Seamus reunited, and Lucien and Henri joined the family too. Seamus had readily accepted them as his sons as they were Mary's boys, and Mary had accepted all of Seamus's boys with Colleen in turn.

Niall felt like he'd known Lucien—or Luc—forever. Before Lucien had married, Niall had never understood Lucien's belief that he somehow wasn't good enough for Sammie. Now that the tables were turned, Niall had a better inkling of what his brother had gone through and how difficult it must have been to believe himself worthy of his wife's love. Especially now, after Hettie had just rejected Niall.

He stared at his brother for a long moment. "I love Hettie."

Frowning, Lucien shrugged. "Of course you do. You always have." He turned toward the glasses and submerged a few more to soak them in sudsy water, before scrubbing them.

Grabbing his brother's shoulder, Niall spun him, his face flushed and impassioned. "No. I *love* her, like how you love Sammie."

Tilting his head to the side, Lucien did the little shrug he and Henri did that none of the other O'Rourkes did and that Mary said was something they'd learned from their French-Canadian father. "*Oui*, you love her. You always have. This is not news, *non?*"

When aggravated or deeply emotional, Lucien often slipped French words into his speech. "You will marry and be happy." His eyes gleamed. "But you'd better not leave Fort Benton."

Niall took a step back and then another until he collapsed on an empty whiskey barrel. "How can you accept it so readily, when Hettie rejected it?" He looked up to see his brother stare at him sorrowfully. Closing his eyes, Niall rubbed at them and fought to hide the anguish that wanted to spill forth. "She said I only claimed to love her because I hate change. Because I was afraid of losing her to another. That I didn't really love her." His breath caught at understanding the depth of her doubt.

"You do hate change, Niall," Lucien murmured. "For yourself."

Niall shrugged. "Aye. Perhaps Hettie would be better off with a man who …" He rubbed at his forehead.

"*Non*, don't spout that garbage. If you wouldn't let me say it when I wanted Sam, you can't say it now." He looked at his brother and sighed. "You know *she* lied."

Niall nodded, understanding they were no longer talking about Hettie, but his mother, Colleen. "A part of me does. The other part will always believe her."

"Until you know she was wrong, you'll never fight for Hettie the way you should."

Niall stared at Lucien, with bleak comprehension. "Then perhaps it's better I let Hettie go."

Leaning against the rickety counter, Lucien shook his head, as he witnessed his brother's misery. "Only if you want to never know the true meaning of joy." He pushed away and spun to wash dishes. "Come. Help me." He waited until Niall was beside him, before speaking in a soft voice again. "I was smart enough to ignore my father's and my uncle's taunts and to trust in my wife's love. You should be wise and take after me."

Lucien laughed as Niall splashed him with water, and soon they talked about Etienne and Samantha, leaving Niall to ruminate about Hettie on his own.

CHAPTER 6

The following day, Niall waited for Hettie to come to the saloon to clean the rooms or to help with any of the numerous chores that kept the place running. However, she never arrived. Winnie bustled in, with a smile and a wave, moving upstairs to work alone. She didn't give him any odd looks, so he suspected Hettie hadn't said anything to Winnie about what had happened last night.

Lucien sent him a sympathetic glance. "Da wants to see you. At the warehouse."

"What?" Niall sputtered. He knew being summoned to the warehouse and Da's office was never a good thing. Had A.J. told Da about how surly Niall had been last night? Looking around, he saw Bryan and Henri working, as they chattered and helped ready the saloon for opening. "Will you be all right?"

Lucien smiled and nodded at their youngest brothers. "With those two here, I'll be fine. Don't rush back."

Niall nodded, striding out of the saloon and down the boardwalk toward the family's warehouse, behind the family store on Front Street. Although Fort Benton was growing, and now another store competed with theirs, the O'Rourkes never lacked for customers.

Everyone knew they sold only the finest products, and word had spread that purchasing goods from the O'Rourkes ensured quality.

Cutting through an alley, Niall approached the warehouse, pausing to take a deep breath, before pushing inside with a lazy grin, as though he didn't have a care in the world. He called out a greeting to his older brother Kevin and to Oran, the third brother who made up the pack. Oran was the eldest member of the pack and had been working with Kevin for the past four or five years. They kept the warehouse tidy and organized, even with the chaos of constant shipments this time of year.

Kevin made a motion for Niall to head into Da's office, which was off to the side of the warehouse. Poking his head into the room, Niall saw Da's back, as he stood behind his desk, cluttered with papers and invoices. Da stared out the window, lost in thought. "Da?"

Seamus turned at the sound of his voice and smiled. "Ah, lad, 'tis good of you to come visit me." He still stood tall with no stoop to his broad shoulders, although his hair held more gray than black now. His blue eyes were eagle sharp, and he missed little, as he cast a quick glance over his son.

Niall shrugged casually—in an attempt to act like this was a relaxed social call—although he knew he'd been commanded to visit. He'd never point that out to Seamus, as his da didn't like to believe he forced his sons to do anything, now that they were grown men. However, although they all had a say in the running of their businesses, they all looked to Seamus for guidance. He was their patriarch, and they trusted his advice. And, if Niall were honest, Seamus was the one they always looked to for advice and support when things went wrong in every other aspect of their lives, especially the emotional side. "Bryan and Henri are at the saloon, so they can help Luc."

Seamus nodded and motioned for Niall to sit across from him, as he sat at his comfortable chair behind his desk. "Aye, they're good lads, and 'tis about time they had something to do, rather than run around and chatter everyone's ears off with their tales." He smiled, as he considered his youngest sons. "Now what's this I hear about you bein' surly toward customers?"

Niall swallowed a groan and met his da's implacable stare. "I was out of sorts last night, Da. It won't happen again."

Seamus raised an eyebrow. "Last night too?" He shook his head and tapped a finger on a pile of papers. "I was talkin' about a few nights ago." When Niall squirmed, Da nodded. "Seems you can't recall all the times you're actin' inhospitable to our guests." Pinning his son with a severe stare, his blue eyes shining with disappointment, Da said, "For they are our guests. Anyone who's behavin' in our saloon is a guest, Niall. You know that."

Sighing, Niall leaned forward, bracing his elbows on his knees. "I know, Da. You've drummed that in my head enough times. I know I'm supposed to be charming and witty an' not care when ..." He bit back what more he would have said.

"When you meet the man who plans to steal away your love?" Seamus murmured in a soft tone, his gaze now filled with compassion.

Niall deflated even more. "Does everyone know?" He cast a furtive glance to meet his father's gaze, an embarrassed flush reddening his cheeks.

"Nay, lad." Seamus cleared his throat. "I, ... I was about to get your mum her glass of milk, when I heard you and Hettie talkin' last night." He waited, as he saw Niall comprehend what that meant. "I ... heard."

Groaning, Niall leaned forward and rested his forehead on the desk, battling tears of futility. "Do you think like she does? That I look at her like a toy I'm afraid of losing?"

"Niall," Seamus said in a quiet voice, filled with a soft reproach. He waited for Niall to raise his head. "You know better than that, lad. You're a fine, honorable man. You hoped you would have more time before you had to come to terms with what you feel." He paused. "An' you've yet to overcome your mother's ... nastiness."

Niall froze. "What would you know about it?" He rose, wishing he could race from the room. Flee this conversation. But Da would find him and confront him. He had his ways of forcing them to face their worst fears. What a fool Niall had been to believe his da knew nothing of Niall's.

Seamus rose, stilling his approach of his son when Niall tensed. Instead Da perched on the edge of his desk. He appeared calm, although anyone who knew him could sense the tension thrumming through him. "Did you never wonder why her verbal barrage ended when you were nine?"

Niall shrugged. His mother, Colleen, had died when he was twelve, during an outbreak of influenza, leaving Seamus with nine children to again care for by himself. Thankfully his sister Niamh was older and could help tend the house, and they all took turns cooking and cleaning, as best they could. The adventure to travel to Fort Benton had come as they were just emerging from mourning Colleen's loss, although Niall knew his da had never loved his mother the way he loved Mary.

But how could he have? Colleen was miserly with her love, dispensing it like a precious penny to those she considered worthy, rather than lavishing it on everyone, as Mary did. Colleen clung to bitterness and heartache as her fiercest companions and resented any happiness or joy. Colleen had tried to destroy them as a family, and Niall gave thanks every day that she had failed.

"I assumed she grew bored," he finally whispered.

Unable to stay away from his boy for another moment, Seamus approached and squeezed his shoulder. "Nay, lad. Do you not remember me talkin' with you? Tellin' you that I was always proud of you and that I couldn't be more delighted you were my son? That I hoped you'd never doubt joy and laughter and love?"

Niall nodded, his gaze holding the echo of the lost boy he'd been. "Aye, I do," he whispered.

Seamus's eyes gleamed a brilliant blue from the tears he didn't shed. "I heard, Niall. I heard her. An' I'm so damn sorry."

"Da, it was my fault."

"No!" Seamus barked in a harsh rasp. "Don't accept her shameful behavior toward you as something you deserved." He shook his head and then shook it again, as though he could push it away. "She struck out at me in the only way she knew would hurt me." When Niall stared at him in blank confusion, Seamus murmured, "By hurtin' my children."

"Da," Niall croaked.

"I should never have married her, but I can never regret the joy of you and Oran and Bryan." Seamus's gaze glowed with sorrow. "Don't be me, lad. Mournin' the woman of your soul because you lost her. Me from a terrible error. You?" He paused and shrugged.

Niall sniffed and swiped at his nose. "I can't make her love me."

Seamus paused a long moment, staring deeply into his son's eyes. "Do you refer to your mother or to Hettie?"

Lifting one shoulder in a hopeless shrug, Niall sighed. "Either. Both." He closed his eyes. "You never called her mum. Never."

Clearing his throat, Seamus dropped his gaze and flushed, as he battled a personal shame. "Mary was *Mum*. She was the one who knew what it was to love and cherish and adore. Not Colleen." He dropped his hand from Niall's shoulder and spun away, massaging the nape of his neck. "Perhaps the fault was in me. I didn't inspire it in her the way I did in Mary. Or ..."

"Maybe it only happens when there is love between the two," Niall whispered.

"Perhaps." Seamus stared at his son for a long moment. "Don't accept what Hettie said last night as truth. I heard fear more than anything in what she said."

Niall paced around the office. "How do I prove that I love her? Shouldn't she know it?" He stared at his father, as a terrible fear filled him. "What more can I do?"

Smiling at his son, he chuckled. "Ah, lad, you've never *woo*'d her. That's entirely different."

Freezing, Niall was dumbstruck. "*Woo?*" he breathed. "I have to woo her? Show her what she means to me?"

"Aye, an' I've found little notes are often appreciated." He squeezed Niall's arm, before he returned to sit behind his desk.

"Thanks, Da." Niall shared a long look with his father, as words seemed insufficient for everything he wanted to say. When his da looked at him in complete understanding, Niall heaved out a breath of relief. "For now, I'd better return to help Luc."

As he wandered back to the saloon, his mind was filled with possibilities for ways to woo his Hettie. He only hoped she'd believe him.

～

Hettie rushed to Niamh's house, as she'd received a message that Niamh needed help with her children. After knocking once, she poked her head inside, confused to find the house tidy and quiet. Where were Niamh and Cormac's children?

"Niamh?" she called out, smiling when Niamh bustled out of the rear bedroom she shared with her husband. "Is everything all right?"

Grinning at her, Niamh smiled. "Aye, all is well. I thought I'd be run off my feet today, but Theresa just came by and took the children to Lorena's. They'll have a wonderful time playing with their cousins, and I now have time for a chat and a cup of tea with you."

"Oh, I couldn't," Hettie protested. "There's too much work to do at the café and ..."

Niamh shook her head, waiting until Hettie's protests died away. "I know all about how hard you work. We all do. But Deirdre and Mum won't mind if you take a few moments to sit with me."

Somehow, within a few minutes, Hettie was seated at the dining room table, a delicious slice of tea cake and a cup of tea in front of her, while Niamh sat across from her, ready for a chat. How had this happened?

"I heard from Mum you have a suitor," Niamh said, with a delighted smile. "What's he like?"

"Jacob?" Hettie asked, forcing her mind away from Niall and the passionate embrace she'd shared with him the night before. "Kind. Nice. Attentive."

Niamh frowned, wiping at her lip after taking a bite of cake, as she studied Hettie. "You don't sound delighted he's taking you out to dinner."

Flushing, Hettie shrugged. "I'm not the sort of woman ..." She broke off what more she would have said. She wanted to be that sort of woman. She wanted to delight in the man she was with. She wanted him to feel the same for her.

Niamh made a small sound of distress, as she traced the edge of her cup with a finger. "I remember what it was like to be swayed by fancy words and sweet promises. I remember believing I didn't deserve more." Her gaze held a warning, as she stared at Hettie. "Don't make the mistakes I made."

"I'm sure I don't—"

Reaching forward, Niamh grabbed Hettie's hand, before she could jerk away and race from the room. "No, you do. You believe, for whatever reason, that you don't deserve my family's love. That you should always stand to the side and find a way to be useful. That we couldn't possibly care for you because of who you are."

Hettie gaped at her.

"We all have to work hard to survive, but working hard doesn't determine your lovability, Hettie." Niamh's words were soft but cut Hettie to the bone. "We care for you because you're a wonderful person, kind, loyal, funny, and you fill our homes with joy every time you enter them." She nodded when Hettie stared at her in shock, fighting tears.

"If you don't care for Niall, we will all be saddened, but we will understand. You can't force love. But, if you're denying yourself a chance with a man, like my brother, simply because you are afraid or you believe you're not worthy ..." Niamh shook her head, and her gaze was mournful. "I'd hoped he'd be with someone more courageous."

"I have plenty of courage," Hettie snapped. "I survived!"

"Surviving and thriving are two very different things."

Hettie froze at Niamh's words, her eyes widening in shock. Snatching her hand out of Niamh's hold, Hettie stumbled to her feet, muttering her thanks for the tea before she left. She rushed away, wishing she could believe all the O'Rourkes felt like Niamh.

Instead all Hettie felt was turmoil and an unremitting uncertainty.

CHAPTER 7

The following evening Hettie sat on the front steps, waiting for Jacob. She didn't want him to suffer any more interrogations by O'Rourke family members, even if they claimed they were looking out for her. She'd been successful in avoiding Niall the past few days, and Deirdre had been kind enough to not ask any questions about Jacob or the dinner Hettie had shared with him.

Hettie tried to ignore the impromptu tea she'd had with Niamh, but Niamh's advice about thriving rather than merely surviving played through her mind. It was a subtle taunt that she was accepting too little from her life. She was acting like a coward, but she didn't know where she would find the courage to reach for what she most wanted.

Trying to relax, she rested in the shade of the front porch, knowing questions were inevitable now that she would have her second dinner with Jacob at the café. However, she had agreed to eat there again because it was the best place in town and because Ardan was discreet. If she ate in the other café, she suspected Niall or another O'Rourke would sit at the table beside hers and listen in on everything they discussed.

"Why the sigh, Miss Henrietta?" Jacob stood in front of her, looking handsome in a fine black suit with a cranberry waistcoat and with the gold chain to a pocket watch visible. He looked every bit a successful businessman.

Hettie startled at the sound of Jacob's deep baritone and then laughed. "Oh, I was imagining if we went to the other café. The horrible food and the spies the O'Rourkes would plant to ensure I was well treated." She flushed, as she belatedly realized she'd just insulted him. "They're overprotective."

He smiled and gave no indication that he was offended. "With good reason. They care for you like one of their own. From what I've learned during my short time in town, they're good people." At her nod, he motioned for her to rise and hooked out his arm for her to slip her hand through.

As they started to walk, he spoke in a soft tone that she found soothing. "However, I'd like to do what you want. Would you rather go to the other café? The O'Rourkes wouldn't know of our change of plans, and we'd have more privacy."

Hettie giggled and shook her head, her eyes glowing with mischief and delight. "No, let's go to the O'Rourke café. Deirdre's food is delicious, and Ardan will give us a secluded table again. Besides, if we didn't arrive, they'd send out a search party."

He smiled. "To the O'Rourke Café it is. Did you help prepare tonight's feast?"

She met his smile and nodded. "Yes. I enjoy working with Deirdre, and we always sing and talk. Time passes quickly."

Soon they were seated at the same table as two nights before, waiting for Ardan to bring them glasses of water. The special was fried chicken, mashed potatoes, pickled beets, and corn bread.

"Save room for dessert," Hettie murmured. "Deirdre made delicious chocolate cake this afternoon because it was a little cooler than usual." She saw his eyes light up. "You like cake?"

He grinned at her. "I do. I also like whatever gives you that sparkle." When she blushed, he smiled broadly. However, when Ardan emerged from the kitchen with bowls of soup for them, Jacob leaned back and pasted on a more somber expression.

Hettie played her spoon through the hot liquid, ostensibly to cool it, but really to calm her nerves. "What did you do today?"

"I wandered around town, listened to men boast and tell tales that are too fantastic to believe. And meandered into the little bookshop down from the main road. I had the most fascinating conversation with the woman who owns it."

"Lorena?" Hettie asked, with raised brows. "Why was it fascinating?"

He shrugged. "I don't believe that was her name. This woman was older and had an encyclopedic knowledge of books. She was fascinating to talk with, but she never made me feel uneducated for not having read as much as she had."

Hettie set down her spoon, as a fond expression flitted over her face. "Oh, that was Mrs. Pickens. Missus Bessie. She's a treasure. She moved here around the time I arrived, and she's like an aunt to all the O'Rourkes. Her husband was a steamboat captain, and he befriended the O'Rourkes on some of his travels up the river, years before he and Bessie moved here."

Jacob pushed away his empty soup bowl and nodded. "She's an adventurous woman to give up her life in Saint Louis for the unknown here, but she seems to be thriving." He reached forward and squeezed Hettie's free hand on the table.

She gazed at his hand on hers but didn't move her hand from under his. It felt comforting and secure, although her breath didn't catch with anticipation like it did when she touched Niall. Instead it was … pleasant. Swallowing, she wondered if it could ever grow into something more than that. Should she want anything more than that?

Forcing her way free of her thoughts, she added, "Missus Bessie is enjoying Fort Benton. She tells stories as much as Mr. A.J. does, and she doesn't seem to miss Saint Louis."

When Ardan appeared to remove their soup bowls and returned soon afterward with their suppers, Jacob sighed, as he had to release her hand. "Do you miss Saint Louis? Your family there?"

She swallowed and shook her head. Although she'd told him a few stories about her early childhood, she'd refrained from telling him much about her life. Flushing, she murmured, "I have no one to miss. I was an orphan, and I'd lived by my wits for too long. Winnie, Winnifred O'Rourke, and I became friends, and I traveled here with her. I had nothing to lose."

"And everything to gain," he teased, the soft rumble of his laugh making her blush even more. Sobering, he gazed deeply into her eyes. "I'm sorry you were alone in the world and thankful they were generous enough to take you in."

"Me too." She cleared her throat and focused on the meal in front of her. She preferred not to think about that time in her life, when she was alone and desperate. Or the lies she consoled herself with about the realities of her past.

"I would have thought one of their sons would have married you by now."

"Oh, well, we're friends." Her protestations sputtered out, and she took a deep breath. "Niall and I are close, but he's always seen me as a sister."

"*Hmm,*" Jacob murmured, as he focused on his meal.

Hettie ate much more slowly than he did, and, when he had just about finished his meal, she asked, "What about you? Won't you tell me something more about your life, before you traveled here? I know a little about your youth but nothing else."

He nodded. "You've earned that right." He cleared his throat and took a sip of water. "I was married before." He waited, as though expecting a barrage of questions. When none came, he relaxed. "We had a son. A beautiful boy who was curious about everything. His favorite thing was butterflies." His smile faded, and he stared at her with anguish and regret in his gaze. "I was a man of business in New York City. Always busy. Always trying to better myself for them." He cleared his throat again and took another sip of water. "There were days I thought myself too busy for frivolous trips to the park."

Hettie nodded, her focus wholly on him, as she set down her silverware and reached her hand out to squeeze his. "What happened?"

"It was a spring day, like any other. Sunny and warm, and I knew tomorrow would be just as nice. Tomorrow I'd go to the park with them." He shook his head. "But there was no tomorrow. Their carriage crashed, and they died. Crushed before anyone could save them." He looked at her, his gaze filled with self-loathing. "And I wasn't there."

"Jacob," she whispered.

"Don't," he breathed. "Don't say, *It's not my fault.* Don't say, *I couldn't have known.* Don't say, *You're certain they didn't suffer.*" His blue eyes sparkled with unshed tears and self-loathing. "I decided work was more important than them, and I lost them."

She sat in stunned silence for a long moment, her food forgotten in front of her. "Is that why you left? Why you decided to come here?"

He nodded. "It's been three years, but I needed a new start. I needed to get out of our home. Away from a place where memories were around every corner." Letting out a deep breath, he looked at her with frank honesty. "I want to start again."

Hettie nodded, her compassion warring with her common sense. "I understand."

He studied her for a long moment. "Do you?" He leaned forward, his voice dropping to nearly a whisper, so only she heard what he had to say. "I can't promise you anything, Henrietta, except that I will be faithful and trustworthy and kind. I'll never raise a hand to you. And you'll never worry about being poor."

Hettie forced a smile to confirm she'd heard him, but her mind raced. He'd just told her, in the politest way possible, that he couldn't love her. Would he ever love her? Was there any hope? She closed her eyes, as Niall's emphatic declaration from a few nights ago washed over her, and she shivered. In an instant, everything was so much more complicated than she'd ever imagined.

Suddenly there was the real possibility of not being truly loved by either man.

Pushing thoughts that terrified her from her mind, she murmured, "Let's enjoy our cake and our evening." She entertained him with stories about the young O'Rourke children and listened to him talk about his travels here. Through it all, a deep despair had begun to fill her, and she was more confused than ever.

~

Hours after returning home, Hettie sat in the large O'Rourke family kitchen, thankful it was empty. She hadn't bothered to light a candle, and the moonbeams filtered in through the windows, casting just enough light so she wouldn't bump into anything. She'd returned home after walking with Jacob to find that Ardan had delivered the leftovers of her meal, leaving them in the icebox for her.

Now ravenous, she ate with abandon, devouring the rest of her fried chicken dinner. With a satisfied sigh, she sat back and wiped her mouth with her napkin, as she sipped at a glass of milk and thought about the evening. After her dinner with Jacob, they'd walked around town, before he escorted her home and gave her a kiss on her hand.

After hearing his story, she better understood his reticence and why he didn't attempt to kiss her. Running her hands over her lips, she wondered what it would be like. Would he kiss her like Niall had? Like he were a starving man and he couldn't survive without her? Or would it be a soft peck on her lips? Would she feel like she had fire in her veins or only a mild interest?

She sat, her gaze unfocused, as she relived that moment with Niall two nights ago. The absolute wonder of being in his arms. Of feeling, just for a moment, that he desired her as much as she wanted him. Then she'd been reminded of why he was desperate for her not to leave, and she'd been just as desperate to escape him. She wasn't strong enough to handle him not truly loving her.

Coward, she whispered to herself, and she ducked her head, acknowledging she was giving in to her worst fears. Her fear of being abandoned. Of finding herself alone again. Of daring to dream and having those dreams destroyed. She swiped at her cheeks, fearing she wasn't as strong as she needed to be to dream for a future with Niall.

"Who hurt you, lass?" Niall asked.

Gasping, her head jerked up, and she met his concerned stare, his face half in shadow, half in light. The one eye she saw clearly was lit with a murderous rage. Unthinkingly she reached forward and gripped his hand. "No one."

"You sit alone in the kitchen, after a midnight snack, crying every night?" He frowned as though attempting to puzzle out a mystery. "I know Mum likes her milk, but I never realized you liked to eat so late."

Giggling, she shook her head and stared at him in wonder for a moment. "No. I didn't eat much at supper, and Ardan brought over my leftovers. When I couldn't sleep, I was ravenous, so I ..." She broke off what more she would have said, as his eyes lit with desire and longing at the word *ravenous.* "I should go to bed."

"No, Hett." He reached for her, swearing softly when she cried out in pain as his fingers gripped her forearm. "I didn't grab you that hard. Forgive me."

"It's nothing."

Looming over her, he held her shoulders in his hands and shook his head, staring at her ominously. "Don't lie to me, lass. Who hurt you?" When she refused to answer, he growled out, "If it was that bastard who thought to charm you, he's a dead man."

As he spun away to storm out and find Jacob, Hettie cried out, "No!" She launched herself at his back. Wrapping her arms around his waist, she held on, pressing against him. She felt him shudder in her arms, and she shivered at feeling his latent strength. Did all men have so many muscles on their backs? "I forbid you."

He eased out of her hold and turned to look at her, moving them until they both stood in a shaft of moonlight. His eyes glowed with molten fury for being denied his right to defend her. "You'd forbid me? From protecting you from a man who hurt you?"

A tear trickled down her cheek as she stared at him, more confused than ever. Was this out of brotherly concern or something more? Oh, why couldn't she tell? "He didn't do anything to me." She nodded at him earnestly, when his glower intensified. "Someone else did."

He clamped his jaw shut, and it looked like he wanted to roar. Instead he rasped, "Tell me."

Her voice quavering, she said, "Aileen's aunt. Mrs. Davies."

He swore softly and eased loose the button on the cuff at her wrist, pushing up the sleeve. Angling her arm so it was in the moonlight, he saw the faint bruises, and he traced each one. *"Jaysus,* lass," he breathed, just a second before he dropped his head and kissed them, evoking a shiver at his soft, reverent touch. "I'm sorry she hurt you. She had no right."

Watching him, Hettie fought a nearly overwhelming urge to sob. To pull him to her and to beg him to never let her go. Instead she swallowed and tugged gently on her arm. "I'll be fine. They barely hurt."

Her breath caught when he took the step that separated them, cradling her face in his large calloused hands, his thumb caressing the soft skin of her cheek. "Lie to yourself if you must, but not to me. Never to me."

She shuddered, blinking her agreement, speech beyond her ability.

Leaning forward, he kissed her forehead. "I love you, Hettie. Somehow, someway, I'll prove to you that I'm telling the truth." He ran his lips over her soft skin one more time, before he backed away, stepped around her, and moved silently from the room, leaving her devastated and confused.

Her fingers trembled as they rose to touch her forehead, and she closed her eyes, memorizing the feel of nearly being in his arms again. Sniffing, she could still smell his subtle scent of cologne, sweat, and whiskey.

Holding a hand to her stomach, she wished she knew what to do. Thankfully she still had a little more time to decide.

CHAPTER 8

The following day Ardan poked his head into the saloon and met Niall's gaze. Niall looked at Lucien, patted his brother on the back, and walked out the front door for a quick chat with his eldest brother. Thankfully the saloon wasn't very busy, and Henri and Bryan worked there every day now. Although they were sometimes rambunctious and had to be set loose to run around and to get rid of excess energy, they were hard workers and always a joy to be around.

Niall fell into step beside his eldest brother, a man he respected nearly as much as Da. When they reached a quieter area a short distance from the levee on the banks of the Missouri River, Niall let out a deep breath and waited. Ardan would say what he wanted to when he was ready. For now, Niall would enjoy a few minutes outside.

Today was scorchingly hot, even too hot for birds to swoop and chirp as they hunted insects, and the prairie grass had already been burned a pale gold in the hot sun, as it now swayed in the faint breeze. Although only early July, the river was almost too low for steamboats to reach town, and soon they'd have to dock downstream at Cow Island, with the men ferried by stagecoach to Fort Benton and then onward into the Territory.

"Why is Hettie having meal after meal with that man?" Ardan asked. He stood beside Niall, staring out at the river, as though he didn't have a care in the world. Niall supposed Ardan didn't. He was married to the woman of his dreams and had a beautiful four-and-a-half-year-old son named Rory. What more could Ardan want?

"I can't tell her that she can't have dinner with him." He flushed when Ardan stared at him like he was an idiot.

"You can show her why she shouldn't want to have dinner with any man but you." He spoke in his deep voice, with the soft lilting sound of Ireland in it, a voice Niall had mimicked when he was a boy.

"I've tried, Ard. She doesn't believe me when I tell her that I love her. She gets prickly when I touch her." He suddenly felt like crying, so he slammed a fist against his thigh to feel a different sort of pain. The heartache was almost too much to bear. "She's turned against me for some reason."

Heaving out a sigh, Ardan slung an arm around his brother's shoulders. "I know this torment well. Your Hettie is afraid, Niall. You have to show her why she's wrong. And let her go, if she's determined to leave."

Frowning at his brother's words, Niall shook his head. "You didn't let Deirdre go. You chased after her."

"Aye, I did. And then, once we were back in Fort Benton, I had to let her go. Her fears were almost too big for us. I had to let her overcome them, without me pestering her."

Niall stared out at the river, moving at an unrelenting pace from the mountains toward a distant place he would never see. "I have to show her that I'm sincere? And let her go if she wants to leave?"

"Aye," Ardan murmured, squeezing Niall's shoulder once, before quietly striding away.

Niall remained standing, hypnotized by the river, as he considered what Ardan had said. Although Niall agreed with his brother, he knew he wouldn't give up on Hettie without a fight. And, even if she left, he'd never stop praying that she'd return to him.

~

Henrietta returned to her bedroom at the O'Rourke house, desperate for a few minutes to herself. She had successfully avoided Niall for the past few days, although he'd always been in her thoughts. How could he not be?

He left her little trinkets of affection everywhere. At the café, he left a new paring knife he hoped would help her work in the café, with a note that simply read *I hate to see you harmed, N.* How many times had he teased her about the knicks and cuts she'd inflicted on herself, while paring vegetables and chopping them up?

Then she'd found a handwritten copy of one of her favorite sonnets on her pillow, with another note. *Something to dream about tonight, N.* Of course she'd spent the night, tossing and turning, her dreams filled with her wildest imaginings for a future with Niall. A future she should know better than to long for.

Today she stopped short upon entering her room to see a bouquet of wildflowers on her pillow. Her hand shook, as she reached for the card. *To brighten your room as you brighten my life, N.*

With a stifled cry, Hettie collapsed to the floor, a sob escaping. Why was he doing this to her? Why couldn't he just let her go? He couldn't love her, not the way she needed him to. Not the way she loved him. It was all a game. Wasn't it?

When a soft hand stroked over her back, she flinched and gasped out, "I'm fine."

"Ah, lass, you're far from fine," Mary murmured, edging onto the floor and tugging Hettie into her arms. "What's the matter, little love?"

Mary's gentle words only made Hettie sob harder, as she barely remembered her mother's love, but what she did remember was just like Mary's. Warm and kind and gentle. The kind of love that soothed wounds and doled out hugs as readily as a smile and made everything better. Until that last day and the worst betrayal of all.

"I shouldn't talk to you about it," Hettie stammered.

"Ah, 'tis about Niall," Mary said in a soft voice.

Hettie wriggled away from Mary and stared up at her in amazement. "How do you know that?"

"I'm his mum, love." Mary swiped a hand over Hettie's wet cheek and smiled softly at her. "He's been miserable the last week. Ever since Bryan's birthday party." She paused and spoke in a soft voice, "Ever since he learned about your Jacob and your plans to leave us."

Fresh tears coursed down Hettie's cheeks, and she swiped at her nose with her handkerchief. "How do you know that?" she gasped out again, amazed at all Mary knew.

"We do talk, Hettie," she said in a teasing, yet slightly chastising tone. "Seamus and I." Taking a deep breath, Mary gazed at her solemnly. "You must have known how upset Niall would be when another man came to take you out to dinner."

"He only sees me as a sister," Hettie insisted, although her words sounded hollow to her own ears.

Making a *tsk*ing noise, Mary leaned against the side of the bed. "Is that so? Does a brother badger Declan to help him find the loveliest sonnet? Or traipse around searching for wildflowers in the midst of a drought, during the few hours he has free from the saloon, determined to find beauty for the woman he adores?" She motioned to the bouquet of flowers resting on Hettie's bed.

Mary stared at Hettie for a long moment. "Do you feel the same about him? Or is it you who lacks those feelings for him and is feelin' guilty? You should know, lass, there's no shame, no matter how you feel."

Hettie nodded, taking a deep breath.

"However, there is shame, Hettie, in hiding behind your fears and in not letting what you feel for him be more than what you've known —and in denyin' him the chance to show you what he's only just discovered himself. 'Tis cowardly, an' I'd hoped for a stronger woman for my son." She swiped at Hettie's head, her soft touch taking the sting out of her words.

Ducking her head, Hettie fought another sob. "I am cowardly. I'm so afraid." When Mary didn't press Hettie to explain, she felt compelled to tell Mary. For reassurance or understanding, Hettie didn't know which. But she trusted Mary would honor her confidence. "It's easier to believe he sees me as his sister or cousin, than to believe he could love me like I do him."

"Why?" Mary whispered, her hazel eyes shining with concern.

"If I love him so much, and he dies ..." Hettie bit her lip, as tears coursed down her cheek. "Or if I loved him more and ..." She shrugged. "I couldn't bear it."

Mary groaned as she shifted, so she could clasp Hettie's hands. "I lost everyone, Hettie. I lost all my children and Seamus. Everyone except for Maggie." Her eyes shone with the unfathomable grief. "Not once did I regret a single memory or moment I had with them. Not once did I wish I'd married another and had lived a different life. I accept the pain, every minute of it, to have the joy in my life now. To have known the joy then."

She took a deep breath and smiled tremulously at Hettie. "You can't forsake today's happiness over fear of what might come, lass. You have to be brave and have to believe you are strong enough to face whatever might come."

Speaking in a soft voice, Hettie murmured, "I don't trust the constancy of his love. I fear it's only because another has shown an interest in me."

Sighing, Mary heaved herself up, groaning as her body cracked with the movement. Looking down at the younger woman who remained on the floor, she shook her head. "If you truly believe that, after these last four years of his constancy and devotion to you, then you don't know Niall at all. And you don't deserve him or his love."

Hettie sat with her arms wrapped around her legs, as she watched Mary slip from the room.

That evening Niall moved out of the shadows, stepping in front of Jacob as he departed the large O'Rourke home. Niall had felt like the lowliest man, watching this man flirt and talk with Hettie, but Niall had convinced himself that he was watching out for her. That she needed someone to guard against a man who'd take liberties.

When all Jacob had done was kiss Hettie on her hand, Niall had frowned. What kind of man only wanted to kiss Hettie like that? Why wouldn't he haul her into his arms and kiss her until next week?

Pushing aside those thoughts, Niall met the man's startled gaze and matched his movements, so he couldn't step around him. "You're courting Hettie."

Jacob furrowed his brows and tilted his head, as he stared at Niall for a long moment. "You're an O'Rourke. I saw you that first day I took out Miss Henrietta." At Niall's nod, Jacob studied him, with an assessing glance. "You don't have to skulk around, Mr. O'Rourke. I'll never hurt her."

"Words seem to come easily to a man like you. You've sweet-talked Hettie in a matter of days." Niall shook his head, as he leaned forward and dropped his voice to a low growl. "You should leave her alone and go find some other woman to bother."

Chuckling, Jacob rocked back on his heels and stared at Niall, like he was a puzzle. After a long moment, Jacob's expression cleared, and he murmured, "Ah, I understand. You're angry because I was man enough to go after what I wanted and didn't waste my chance." He patted Niall on the shoulder, ignoring that Niall's muscles bunched. "You have my sympathy. She's a remarkable woman, and you're a fool to let her get away."

"And you're a fool to think she'll go with you," Niall snapped. "She has family here."

Just as Jacob was about to walk past him, he spun to face Niall again. "Does she? Or do you believe she should feel that way because you do?" He waited, an impudent smile on his face. "You think you know everything about her, but I doubt you do, Mr. O'Rourke."

Niall watched Jacob stroll away, whistling a jaunty tune, and Niall wanted to beat him to a pulp. However, the man had done nothing wrong. By all accounts, he'd treated Hettie well. According to Ardan, Jacob made her laugh at dinner. A.J. had shared how Jacob had walked her around town and had protected her from leering men. And then Niall had seen for himself how Jacob had only kissed her on her hand.

Rubbing a hand over his face, Niall wondered if he were going mad. Niall wanted to discover Jacob Morrissey was a villain, but he feared Jacob was exactly as he appeared: a lonely wealthy man, searching for a woman to love.

Niall hissed out a frustrated breath and returned to the saloon, determined to forget about his troubles, if only for a few hours. He feared that was a futile hope, but he clung to it.

～

H ettie knocked on Winnie's door, thankful for the few hours of free time. There was always more work to be done, but Deirdre had seen how absentminded and fidgety Hettie was and had urged her to go see Winnie. Winnie and Finn had a small cabin near the other O'Rourke cabins, constructed three years ago. They'd moved in just before Winnie had her baby girl, Ava, and had lived here ever since. Although Finn grumbled sometimes about living away from the café and the ready supply of food and the good advice from his brother Ardan, it was plain to everyone that Finn relished having his own home, rather than living in the rooms above the café with Ardan's family.

Hettie knocked again and then poked her head inside. Winnie was curled on the bed, fast asleep, with little Ava nowhere in sight. Knowing the O'Rourkes, Hettie suspected Ava was off with the other O'Rourke children, playing right now, giving Winnie time to clean, wash, and prepare supper. Hettie never expected to find her asleep. "Shoot," she whispered.

Rather than wake her friend, she closed the front door softly and sat in one of the comfortable rocking chairs on the front porch, thankful for the shade. Her stomach knotted, as she battled indecision, and she wished someone would tell her what to do.

Looking up, she paled. The Madam, dressed in a bright aquamarine dress that sparkled in the brilliant sunlight, walked in her direction, with a look of fierce determination. Although Madam Nora was friends with the O'Rourkes, Hettie had always felt intimidated by the forthright woman and had evaded any contact with her. Now she was face-to-face with the woman who ran Fort Benton's most successful house of ill repute, the Bordello.

Standing only slightly taller than five feet tall, she commanded respect and reluctant admiration from Hettie. Nora had survived and thrived in a world dominated by ruthless men. Meeting Madam Nora's disapproving stare, Hettie said in a low voice, "She's asleep. Winnie. You'll have to come back."

Smiling subtly, Nora chuckled and ascended the steps to the porch, settling in the rocker beside Hettie. "It's fortunate for me. I came to seek you out. Imagine my surprise to see you sitting here all alone, without something industrious taking up your time." She raised an eyebrow, as her brown eyes were filled with mocking humor. "You have a penchant for always remaining busy."

"I am useful," Hettie snapped, before ducking her head and digging her fingernails into palms.

"Ah, is that what you call it? Useful?" Madam Nora kicked the rocker into motion with one foot and rested her hands, one crossed over the other, on her belly. "I thought it was out of a desperation to be proven worthy, so you wouldn't be tossed out."

Her words hit a little too close to home, and Hettie flinched.

When Nora saw her reaction, her expression softened. "You don't have to earn love, Hettie. You just have to *be*. And now it appears you have two fine men vying for you. I only hope you choose wisely."

"What would you know about choosing wisely?" Hettie glared at the older woman, who seemed content with her life.

Studying the younger woman, Nora's deep-brown eyes glinted with the echo of pain for a brief moment. "I know what it is to choose and to choose wrongly. I know what it is to then have no choice other than the only path left for me. I know what it is to have no one there to support me after ... what choice I'd had, had been stripped from me." She leaned forward, her fervent stare pinning Hettie in place. "What do *you* want?"

A tear leaked down Hettie's cheek. "I think—"

Nora reached forward and gripped her hand, giving it a gentle squeeze. "No, Hettie. What do you want? What does your heart want?"

"It's not that simple." Tears cascaded down her cheek.

"Yet it is." She met Hettie's stormy gaze and smiled softly. "Imagine your life, when you're Mary's age, and you have children and grandchildren around you. Who do you want beside you?" She squeezed her hand once and then released it. "Be brave enough to trust and to believe you deserve what the O'Rourkes have. Be brave enough for a man like Niall."

Hettie sat in stunned silence, as she watched Nora walk away. It couldn't be that simple. Her head and her heart continued to battle each other, and she didn't know which one to trust. She tried to envision herself when she was Mary's age, but all she felt was a warm glow. She had children and grandchildren around her, but the man about to enter the room was a mystery.

Sighing, she swiped at her cheeks and rubbed at her forehead. Rising, she peeked inside to see Winnie was still asleep. With a reluctant shrug, Hettie returned to the café, with even more to consider after her discussion with Madam Nora.

CHAPTER 9

Tonight Hettie had been unable to get out of work at the busy supper hour, so she slipped outside a little after eight, when most of the dishes had been cleaned and dried. A few stragglers remained in the café, and Ardan said he'd wash up after he closed.

Letting out a deep breath and arching her back, Hettie closed her eyes for a moment, as the early evening sun warmed her. The sun wouldn't set for nearly another hour, and she felt safe walking the short distance home. When she opened her eyes, she flushed to find Jacob watching her, with a warm smile. "Sir!"

"Miss Henrietta."

His voice sounded like warm chocolate, rich and decadent and slightly sinful. Something she could become addicted to. Flushing at her thoughts, she dropped her gaze and stared at her scuffed boots.

"Have I offended you?"

Her head jerked up, and she shook her head. "No, I wasn't expecting to see you. I was undignified. Unladylike."

He chuckled, approaching her slowly. When he was close, he reached forward and stroked a finger down her cheek, earning a soft shiver. "I saw a woman, giving appreciation for the beautiful weather after a hard day's work. Nothing undignified."

She grinned up at him and looped her hand through his offered arm. "Thank you."

Rather than walk directly toward the O'Rourke house, he circled away, so they'd have a longer distance to walk and more of an opportunity to talk. "How was your day?" he asked, as he tilted his head down toward hers, making a simple gesture feel intimate, as though they were a couple.

She swallowed down panic, as she didn't know what they were. "Good. Deirdre and I work well together. And I managed to have a little time for myself today." She refrained from telling him about her visit with the Madam, as she knew few would find that acceptable.

At her prolonged silence, he asked, "What's bothering you?"

She paused at the levee, now mainly devoid of steamboats, as only the most intrepid captain would dare attempt a journey this far upriver with the water so low. "I've been thinking about our conversation." She met his gaze and saw the concern in his beautiful blue eyes. "I'm still uncertain what I'll do."

He firmed his jaw, and it ticked a few times. "Is it because you believe I'll fail to protect you too?"

"What? No!" She grabbed his arm and squeezed it, her gaze beseeching, as she tried to find a way to express her sincerity, to ease his doubts after suffering the loss of his wife and child. "Never. That's not it at all." She bit her lip and looked down, marshalling all her courage. "I'm trying to determine if I can accept a marriage of friendship and affection." She flushed beet red. "I thought I'd have more."

He nodded. "More," he murmured, looking at her a moment, before glancing away. "I can't promise you more than I am, Henrietta. I can't promise to give you what I know I'll never feel again."

Looking down at her feet, she fought a wave of disappointment. Had she expected him to be passionately enamored of her so soon? "I understand," she whispered. "I ... There's a lot to decide."

Pressing two fingers under her chin, he lifted her head so she'd meet his gaze. "There is, but we don't have much time. I leave in two days."

"So soon?" she gasped. She'd known it was coming fast, but she'd hoped it were different somehow.

He pressed a finger to her lips and smiled. "For now, let's enjoy our walk. Tomorrow we will have supper together again and then …"

"And then …" Hettie whispered, her hand tightening on his arm. She had no idea what she'd decide, but she knew she'd miss his friendship. For, if nothing else, he had become a friend. Was that a terrible basis for a marriage?

She allowed him to urge her into walking, and soon she was laughing at stories from his life in New York City, while she told him about O'Rourke escapades. Through it all, she wished she had a month with him to help her determine what she wanted. Two more days was too little time.

Niall entered the saloon that evening in a foul mood. And then his mood worsened. He had glanced out the front window of the bar during the busiest time and had seen Hettie walking with that weasel. Niall had stormed outside, watching as Jacob lowered his head while they talked, as though no one else existed in the world. Then Niall had stood helplessly as he watched them turn away and walk toward the O'Rourke home.

Niall had pushed down his desire to march toward them, to rip Hettie away from the weasel, and to escort Hettie home himself. He knew that would not have been appreciated. Instead he'd stood in silent misery, while the woman he loved was courted by another man. How could she do this to him?

Later this evening Niall saw Hettie slip out the back door of his family's house and head toward the creek. Glancing at the darkening sky, as the faint pink of the sunset faded, he knew twilight would last for a while in the long Montana summer evening, but he feared she'd linger and attempt to walk home in the dark.

Following after her, when he saw her stop at the place he thought of as the "O'Rourke thinking spot," he grinned. "Hett!" His smile froze, when she glared at him over her shoulder.

"What are you doing, stalking me?"

"Stalking you?" He flushed, as he considered his actions tonight—traipsing around town after her—of protecting her. Niall had felt compelled to ensure this Jacob fellow treated her well. "I'm looking out for you."

She spun to face him, hitting him square in his chest as she pushed at him, forcing him back a step. "How dare you, Niall! I'm not a toy! I'm a grown woman! I don't need you …"

He flushed and leaned over her, his eyes blazing, as his pent-up fury exploded from him. "Do you think I don't know that? You're the gorgeous, maddening woman I'm crazy about!" He flung his arm out, waving toward the town. "And you've made it abundantly clear this past week how you don't need me. How you don't want me. No matter what I say or do, how you'll never believe me. You'll put your faith in a man you've known for days rather than me——a man you've known for years."

He stalked away a step and paced back to her. "No, Hett. You'll allow some man who's just arrived to town to court you. To take you out to dinner, again and again, while ignoring me. Ignoring all the things I do for you, that I've done for you." His breaths heaved in and out, as he shook his head side to side in an agony of hurt. "Does it all mean nothing to you?" He bit back what he truly wanted to ask. Did *he* mean nothing to her?

"Niall, I don't mean to hurt you." She swallowed and closed her eyes.

"You're doin' a piss poor job of it, Hett," he snapped and winced at swearing in front of her. Again. After mumbling his apology, he let out a shaky breath and ran a hand over his face. "How do you think it feels?"

She flinched at his soft question, laced with heartache. Her eyes glowed with sorrow. "Like your world is ending," she whispered and then flushed. "I know what it is to have my world upended, Niall. I know what it is to have no one and to lose everything I ever had faith in. I can't …" She shook her head.

Taking a step toward her, he cupped her cheek, his thumb tracing over her soft skin. "Can't you see I'm as afraid as you, but I'm willin' to take the chance?" He cleared his throat, as hope won against the fear blooming in his chest. "I'm willin' to try."

She gazed up at him, her eyes wide and filled with an unfathomable pain. "I'm not brave like you. I can't base my future on words like *try* and *chance*. I need certainty. I need to know I won't be abandoned …" She broke off what more she would say.

He hissed and yanked her closer, so they were chest to chest, with his head bowed so they shared the same air. "You think I'd abandon you? That I'd ever let anything or anyone harm you? What do you think it means when I tell you that I love you?" Shaking his head, he stared at her, as though she were a stranger. "How could you doubt me so, Hett?"

Pushing at him, she struggled until she was free of his hold. "You don't understand!" she yelled at him, tears now coursing down her cheeks. "You don't understand," she gasped, as she sat down in an ungraceful heap, her skirts all around her.

He knelt beside her, his hands gripping his thighs, rather than reaching out to soothe her as he wished. "I don't, Hett, because you've never explained. You've never told me." His jaw tightened, and a hint of anger laced his tone. "Why have you kept yourself apart? Why have you so selfishly denied my love and the love of my family? Is it because you believe yourself better than us?"

"What?" Hettie breathed, reaching out to grab his hand, shaking her head.

"Is it because we're Irish and you …" He couldn't finish his sentence, hating the thought that Hettie looked down on him and all he loved because of where they were from, because they were peasants and poor immigrants, who'd had to struggle for success.

"Never, no, Niall, of course not!" Hettie cried out.

He sat here, watching as Hettie rocked to and fro, but she didn't say anything more. "Even now, even when you know I adore you, when you know there is nothing you could tell me that would make me *not* love you, you won't tell me the truth."

He froze and stared at her. "Unless you really don't love me." He breathed the words, barely speaking them loud enough to be heard, as though the mere whisper of them were a sacrilege. For living in a world where Hettie didn't love him was unthinkable. Unbearable. His heart splintered at the possibility.

"Niall," Hettie cried out. "No, that's not it. I …" She ducked her head, one hand on her chest, the other on her mouth.

"Or you don't trust me," he murmured. "Either way, it's not enough, is it, Hett?" He rose and stared at the creek in the late twilight. "You want another."

She slapped her hands on the ground, puffs of dust rising before pushing herself up. "I want certainty!" she cried.

Niall turned and stared at her, looking as though he'd aged a decade in the last hour. "There's no such thing in life, Hett." Sighing, he motioned for her to start walking. "I have to return to the saloon, and I refuse to leave you here alone as darkness descends. Come. I'll walk you home."

"Niall," she breathed.

"No, Hett. We've said enough tonight." He walked her to the kitchen door steps, gripping her hand before she raced up them. "We've said enough but one more thing." His eyes glowed with his sincerity. "I love you, Hett. I always will. You might doubt it now, but I'll prove to you my constancy. That I promise."

He raised her hand, kissing it softly, before releasing it and disappearing into the night.

Taking that short break from the saloon to track her to the creek and to have a soul-shattering argument with her was not Niall's plan. Would he never learn?

After returning to the saloon for the remainder of the evening, he'd remembered Da's patience with him, after he was rude to customers earlier in the week. Thus, eager to avoid a true tongue-lashing from his da, Niall forced himself to be polite and even charming to their customers. It almost killed him. By the time they closed and cleaned up, he wished he could drink them out of whiskey or find ten men willing to fight.

Instead Lucien had walked him home, as though he were a two-year-old in need of an escort, and had given him that stare that said, if he went out to pick fights after Lucien left, Lucien would kill him.

So here Niall sat. In the kitchen, yearning for the woman he loved to believe in him. To choose him. To want him with the same burning intensity he wanted her. Instead she was upstairs, most likely dreaming sweet dreams about that weasel who wanted to take her away.

Swearing, he dropped his head onto his folded forearms and let a few of the pent-up tears escape. One shuddery breath and then another, and he promised himself he'd control his emotions before anyone saw how upset he was.

When a soft hand stroked his hair, he jerked upright and spun to stare at the person invading his quiet time. "Mum," he rasped, swiping at his eyes and nose, his face heating up, beet red now to have her see him like this. "I'm just off to bed."

She pressed a hand on his strong shoulder and shook her head. "Sit."

He plopped back down the few inches he'd risen and waited as she rummaged in the icebox for her cup of milk. She loved her mid-evening cup of milk. Often Seamus was sent to fetch it for her, but sometimes she snuck downstairs for it herself. Niall didn't know what was worse: having his da or mum see him like this.

"*Mum*," she murmured. "You've always called me mum. Why is that?"

Niall shrugged. When Mary sipped her milk and waited patiently, he tapped his fingers in front of him, and the rigidity left his shoulders. "She was always *Mother*, never *Mum*. To be a mum, you have to have a softness about you. An ability to love and to love and to love. To find joy in the ridiculous and the profound. To be a champion, even when the one you've loved has failed." He flushed and looked down. "That's what *Mum* means to me."

He waited for her to say something, but when she didn't, he looked up to see her quietly weeping. "Mum? I'm sorry. I didn't mean to upset you. I …" He reached a hand out, uncertain if she wanted him to hug her or not. Why was he so bad at this? Is this why Hettie didn't believe in him?

He ran a hand over his face, wanting to cry as much as his mum was.

"Oh, Niall," she sobbed, as she scooted toward him and wrapped her arms around him. "I've always been your mum. You've been mine since the minute I met you. I'm so proud of you, my boy. My precious boy."

A tear leaked out, and he pressed his cheek to the top of her head, holding her close. "Mum," he whispered. "I'd hear stories from my older siblings. About you and how you'd been. And I dreamed of knowing what that was like."

She eased away, cupping his face. "I'm sorry your mother was unable to show you the love and affection you deserved. She was at fault, Niall, never you. There was never anything lacking in you."

He stared into her hazel eyes a long moment, before suddenly blurting out, "Why did she scream at me that I was unlovable? That no one would ever truly want me? That even my da loathed me because that meant she was bound to him forever? That, if I didn't exist, Da would …" He swallowed and whispered, "Da would have found a way to love her. But I ruined her chance with him."

Mary gasped, her breath hitching with the shock of hearing what Colleen had said. "She dared try to make you feel guilty for your da's inability to love her the way she wanted to be loved?" Cupping his cheeks, she gazed deeply into his eyes, now filled with a mortifying anguish. "Oh, my sweet boy, how terribly cruel of her. None of that was your fault. Seamus could never love her enough because of me. I'm to blame, if there must be blame."

She swiped her fingers over his cheeks and smiled up at him, as her own tears slowly leaked out. "When a man an' a woman love the way your da an' I love each other, 'tis hard to love anyone else after-ward. We were miserable apart."

Niall shrugged, and his gaze dropped. "That's why she was *Mother*, never *Mum*. She had no softness. Not for me."

Mary made an incomprehensible noise and pulled him close, as he cried a little on her shoulder. When he'd calmed, she eased him away, still running a hand over his face and down to his strong shoulders. "Then she was a fool. For I'm so proud of you and filled with such love, every time I look at you."

"I know, Mum," he whispered in a barely audible voice. "I love you too. The best day for this family was the day you arrived. When we found you again."

She smiled impishly. "Aye, for the family. But the best day of *your* life was the day Hettie arrived." When she saw him sober and some of the joy leeched from his gaze, she cupped his cheek. "Fight for her love. She's your match."

Niall sat despondently, and Mary waited until he met her gaze. "Don't let the poison of your mother's words ruin what you could have with Hettie. Colleen lied. You are wanted and lovable." Mary took a deep breath. "Hettie has her own fears. Be brave and share yours with her, before it's too late." Mary kissed his head and rose, leaving him alone to dream and to wonder.

Easing the bedroom door shut, Mary leaned her forehead against it, as she swallowed a sob. She wanted to scream and yell in sorrow and yet dance a jig in joy at the same time. She was such a messed-up mixture of emotions that she didn't know what to do.

"Come to bed, love," Seamus said in a soft, sleepy voice. "I can't rest well if you're not beside me."

When she sobbed and didn't move, he flew from the bed, wrapping his arms around her. "Love? What happened? Who hurt you?"

"No," Mary gasped, turning to press against his chest and to wrap her arms around him. She needed all of his strength right now. "Just hold me."

Seamus bent low, sheltering her as best he could, while she sobbed and sobbed. He kissed her head and neck, ran soothing hands over her back, and waited for the storm to pass. When she calmed, he urged her to their bed, where he curled around her, still holding her in his arms. "There's a love," he whispered, as he kissed her cheek and then her head. "There's my love."

"Seamus, … I love you so much."

"I know, my darlin'. And I you. Why should that have you weepin' like your heart is breakin'?" He leaned up on one elbow, looking down at her in the faint light in the room, his free hand playing over her head and hair.

Her hand rose to play over his face, and she smiled as he turned into her touch. She marveled at how he was always as moved by her soft caress as she was by his. "I went for my glass of milk, and Niall was in the kitchen." Her eyes glowed with unshed tears and grief and joy. "He told me why he never called Colleen *Mum*."

"Aye?"

"He said, to be a mum, in his mind, she has to be someone able to love unconditionally, be soft and kind and …" Her voice broke off, as she stared at Seamus in wonder.

"*You*," Seamus whispered, with a soft, reverent smile.

"Aye," Mary breathed. "I've always considered him one of mine. I'd always hoped he thought himself my son. He does, Shay. He does."

"Oh course he does, *a ghrá*. You've only ever shown him a mum's love." His thumb played over her cheek. "You know no other way to be, my love." He whispered the endearment this time in English, rather than Gaelic.

Taking a stuttering breath, she dropped her hand to grip her husband's shoulder, as though needing his strength to bolster hers. "He told me what Colleen said." Now she stared at her husband with unveiled rage. "How could a woman speak to her child as she did?"

"Tell me what he said, lass. I heard a bit when he was a boy, but not all of it. Don't spare me."

Mary closed her eyes and took a deep breath, only opening them to meet her husband's intense gaze as he pressed a finger under her chin. "She said he was unlovable. That he'd ruined her chances of ever earning your love by being born. That you'd felt bound to her by duty and not love, and you resented her, and him, for it."

Seamus swore under his breath and hauled Mary close, until she was wrapped, arms and legs around him. He shuddered as he held her. "I thought I had protected them from her. I thought lettin' her scream an' rail at me would rid her of the venom that filled her."

"That kind of poison is boundless." Mary wrapped him tighter, holding him as close as she could. "They were lies then, and they're lies now, *a chuisle.*" Mary relaxed, when she felt the terrible tension thrumming through him ease at her calling him *her heartbeat.* It had been her special endearment for him since they were young and in love in Ireland.

"Aye. I hope Niall has the good sense to ignore them."

She pressed a kiss to his chest and smiled. "I hope he has the good fortune to find and to not lose what we have."

"Aye," Seamus breathed, holding Mary tight for long moments, thankful for every moment he held her in his arms.

CHAPTER 10

The next morning Hettie woke early. Tonight she would say goodbye to Jacob, as he didn't want her to be at the carriage tomorrow morning. She attempted to focus on him and on the sorrow to come of missing him. She couldn't. Her mind was filled with Niall and their argument last night.

Pushing out of bed with a huff, she rose, dressing quickly, and snuck down the stairs. She knew Mary would be in the kitchen, preparing breakfast, but Hettie had no desire to see anyone. Instead she crept out the front door, thankful the floorboards didn't creak, and the door closed softly behind her. Taking a deep breath, she looked around the quiet street, as it wasn't yet 7:00 a.m. Walking in the direction of the café, she stilled when she heard her name called.

"Miss Hettie! Don't act like you can't hear me! I know when a woman's actin' deaf, an' when she's up to no good."

She turned and smiled at Mr. Pickens in what she hoped was a disarming smile but knew she had failed when he shook his head at her and motioned her over to sit on his front porch. Although the summer days were invariably hot, the mornings were still cool, and Hettie had snuck out without a shawl. Shivering, she approached him and gave him a chagrined smile. "I should go to the café."

Huffing out a breath, he yanked a blanket from a basket on the porch and pointed to the other rocking chair. "You should sit yourself down and have a chat with ol' A.J. Been too long since I've had a fair maiden on my porch." He wriggled his eyebrows, as he grinned at her.

She giggled, settling in the rocking chair before snuggling under the blanket, giving a thankful shiver as she pulled it all around her. "I doubt that's true. Your Bessie's here with you."

He chuckled. "You're bright as can be, Miss Hettie." He kicked out his legs, his jaw clamped around his unlit pipe. "Which makes an old goat like me wonder why you've been actin' like a darned fool."

She froze in her rocking, her eyes rounded at his comment. Although A.J. had been seen as part of the O'Rourke family for years now, she'd only ever had casual conversations with him. "You're impertinent."

"Oh, don't go fallin' off a high horse, missy. You might just land in dung, and that ain't ever no fun," he said, with a snort. "You ain't got no more airs and *graceless* than the rest of us lowly born." He gave her a severe look. "Even if you do talk all pretty."

"I never said I was any better than anyone else," she sputtered, before muttering, "*graces.*"

He shrugged and leaned toward her; his gaze wholly focused on her. "Then why're you runnin' away from that boy who's mad for you?" A.J. scrunched his brows up and sighed. "Doesn't make no sense, even if I might seem like a half-wit to you at times."

Even though her nerves were strung tight, she laughed and let out a deep breath. "You're not a half-wit. I fear you're smarter than the rest of us."

He *hmph*ed in agreement. "I'm not about to argue with you." He shook his head. "Now why aren't you plannin' your weddin', rather than gallivantin' about town with that weasel?"

"Jacob's not a weasel," she hissed and then closed her eyes. "I believe he's a good man."

A.J. sat in silence for many moments, his teeth making a *clack*ing sound as he clenched and unclenched his pipe. "Ah, child, you've made me feel my age today." He stared at her with sadness and resignation.

"I don't understand you. I thought I'd be older before I said I didn't understand young people. Guess that's what age does to you. It sneaks up on you, and then suddenly you're old." He shrugged.

Hettie frowned, as she studied A.J. A handsome man at forty-five, she didn't consider him old. He was only a few years older than the eldest O'Rourke sibling, Ardan. "Why do you say you're old?" Confused by the change in topic, she was also grateful for it. She had no desire to think any more about Niall and Jacob. She needed a break from her roiling thoughts.

"Because I don't understand how you can ignore what's right in front of you, missy, and that's making me feel old." He sighed and stared about, watching as the town woke up after another raucous night.

Hettie tensed. "Why does everyone believe they have the right to an opinion?"

"Because we're watchin' you make the biggest mistake of your life out of fear, Miss Hettie, and we don't understand why. What's the boy ever done except prove how much he cares?" A.J.'s brown eyes shone with sincerity. After a long moment, he shook his head. "What are you tryin' to prove, lass?"

"I can be fine on my own!" Hettie rasped as she rose, tossing the blanket to A.J.

"Aye, you can," he murmured, lifting his pipe and waving it around, as he stared at her. "And you'll survive because you're that kind of woman." He shrugged. "Will you wake up one mornin', years from now, dreamin' of what you could have had?"

"And what's that?" Hettie demanded, wanting to stomp her foot in aggravation.

"Everything," A.J. said in a soft voice. "Everythin' you've ever dreamed of—if only you weren't a coward."

Hettie let out a little scream of frustration, hopped off his porch, and marched toward the café, hopeful she received no more *helpful* conversations that day.

∿

That evening, after a stilted supper at the café, Jacob led them to a quiet spot by the river. They were well within view of town and any O'Rourke, who wanted to stand and keep watch, while also feeling like they had a little privacy. A nervous energy thrummed through Hettie, and she didn't know what it meant. Was she excited because soon she'd join Jacob? Was it because she was mourning his departure, and she wouldn't be following him to Helena? Why was she so indecisive?

Jacob stood beside her, staring out across the river to the golden bluffs for a few moments. "I enjoy these times with you, Hettie, when words aren't needed, and we can simply be." He smiled. "You are unlike any woman I've ever met. Too many need to chatter and to fill every moment with words. You are patient and careful with what you say."

Hettie flushed, for what he said was true. She did act that way, unless the person knew her really well. Then she was loud and talkative, and her words ran together. Would she ever feel comfortable enough with Jacob to act like that?

He turned to face her, gripping her hands, as he stared down at her earnestly. "I know you haven't spent much time with me. I know it's presumptuous to believe you'd give up your life here and travel to me. But I will give you a wonderful future, Henrietta. I will always take care of you and will ensure you want for nothing."

His thumb ran over her dried and cracked fingers, from all the washing and scrubbing she'd done. "You'll never have to work this hard ever again. You'll have servants taking care of your every wish."

"Servants?" Hettie whispered, her brows furrowed at the thought. "I ... I had no idea ..."

"I'm a wealthy man. Let me share it with you." When she stared up at him, he ran his thumb over her cheek. "I leave tomorrow, Henrietta. Will you travel to me? Will you be my wife when you do?"

Hettie closed her eyes, as the moment of truth was now upon her. Nothing had truly changed with Niall, and she was torn in a way she never knew she could be. The sensible part of her that had known hunger and fear and desperation demanded that she accept Jacob and relinquish her silly dreams. Meanwhile her heart wept at the thought of giving up Niall. "I haven't decided."

He frowned, the soft breeze blowing his blond hair, as his brilliant blue eyes shone with disappointment. "What more should I have done to prove my sincerity?"

"Nothing," she whispered, reaching forward to squeeze his arm. "I … I think very highly of you, but I fear I would prove a disappointment for you as a wife. This is all so fast."

He smiled, the faint amusement easing the dismay in his gaze. "You could never disappoint me, Henrietta. You are a fine woman. Loyal and kind. A good cook and fond of children. We'd build a good life together."

"Don't you want more?" she asked, flushing at her impertinent question. She'd asked him this before, but she wanted to see if any more depth of emotions filled him. *Needed* to see it.

Taking a step closer, his eyes shone with a passionate intensity. "Of course I do, but I'd never pressure you. I want to only show you respect." He closed his eyes and let out a huff of breath. "Which is a lie. I'm pressuring you right now. Forgive me."

She chuckled and allowed him to tug her into his arms. Wrapping her arms around his waist, she rested her head against his chest. He was taller and leaner than Niall, and he smelled of a spicy cologne with just a hint of soap. She knew if she'd been in a room with a bandanna over her head, she'd be able to tell her two suitors apart every time; they smelled so differently to her.

"I've cared for someone else," she whispered.

"I know," he said in a soft voice, his fingers tracing over her back, as his mouth pressed against the top of her head. "You must decide if he is your past or your future. Only you can, Hettie."

"I can't give you an answer, Jacob." She leaned away to meet his troubled gaze. "I wish I could, but I must consider …"

"I won't wait forever, Hettie," he whispered. "I'll be in Helena." He handed her a bag that *clinked*. "This will cover the stagecoach fare and a hotel room in Helena. Come within a month or don't come."

Feeling momentarily breathless, she accepted the bag from him and nodded. "What should I do with this if I don't come? How do I get it back to you?"

He smiled and ran a finger down her cheek, his smile deepening when she subtly turned into his touch. "Keep it. Consider it a present." Dropping his head forward, he kissed her softly once on the lips and then again. He never attempted to deepen the kiss, instead pulling her into his arms and holding her close once more.

She sighed, resting against him again. "I'll miss you." She heard the soft rumble of his chuckle under her ear.

"Good. That should hasten your travel to me." He eased her out of his arms, kissing her head, before he released her fully.

They walked to the O'Rourke house in silence, her thoughts spinning at the decision she still had to make.

Squeezing her hand, Jacob leaned forward, his forehead pressed softly against hers, his warm breath fanning over her. "Never doubt how much I want to marry you, Henrietta. You are a remarkable woman, and I would be the most fortunate man to call you my wife."

She felt one more soft kiss to her brow, and then he walked away from her. She wanted to call out to him. To beg him not to leave. To take her with him. And just as quickly, she was ashamed of her feelings. Didn't she want Niall? Wasn't it better if Jacob left?

Tears leaked out, as indecision and despair welled forth. She wished she knew what to do, but she knew whatever she did would lead to heartbreak. She only hoped it wouldn't be her heart she tore in half.

Unable to sleep, with her thoughts racing, Hettie slipped from her bed and walked soundlessly downstairs. She knew Mary swore by a cold glass of milk in the middle of the night when she suffered from insomnia, and Hettie wondered if it would help her. Opening the icebox, she removed the jar of milk and poured herself a glass.

Sitting at the table, she stared into space, as she took small sips of milk, her mind racing as she remained uncertain what she should do. Niall pulled at her in a way she had never imagined she'd feel. He made her want to be brave. To believe the disappointments of the past wouldn't repeat themselves.

Closing her eyes, she tried to silence her memories. Instead she saw herself as a girl, barely ten years old, crying out in confusion and desperation. Alone. Terrified. Desperate. Learning too early the meaning of betrayal.

She took a deep breath and froze, smelling the faint scent of cologne, sweat, and whiskey all mixed together. Niall was here. Opening her eyes, she saw him watching her, as he stood in the kitchen shadows. "Niall," she whispered.

"Hello, love," he murmured. "I'm sorry I disturbed you from your waking dream."

Shaking her head, she huffed out an incredulous breath. "I'm not. You saved me from remembering a nightmare." Flushing, she ducked her head, closing her eyes in shame, as she admitted too much.

"Hett," he breathed, taking a step toward her, before stilling. "Forgive me. I'm intruding again where you don't want me."

Gazing at him with confusion, she tilted her head to one side. "Again?"

"Last night. I, ... I should have left you alone at the stream. I ruined everything, and I'm sorry, Hett."

She bit her lip and remained silent, as he clung to the shadows. Niall was meant to be in the light. He was a man who brought joy and was full of life. He'd brought her to life after, ... after ... Her mind shied away from thinking about those years she'd rather forget. "Niall," she whispered, her voice shaking, "you didn't ruin everything." Swallowing, she gathered her courage and whispered, "I fear I can never be who you really need."

Groaning, he strode to her and sat beside her, straddling the bench so he faced her. Lowering his head, his forehead brushed against hers. "You've always been what I needed. I wish I'd realized it sooner. Give me a chance, Hett. Please."

"*Shh*, no begging," she whispered, moving so she could rest in his arms. She shivered as he wrapped her close, his warm breath on her neck evoking shivers of delight. "I'm so scared."

His fingers caressing up and down her back now froze. "Of me?"

"Never," she breathed. "Of me. Of making the wrong choice."

He gripped her closer, and she snuggled in even more, feeling like she was precious and cherished. She never wanted this moment to end. "Only you can decide, Hett." He eased away, his eyes laced with pain and longing, as he brushed a fingertip over her cheek. "I can't make you love me."

She frowned at the uncharacteristic uncertainty in his voice. "No," she whispered. "It's a gift. Freely given."

Smiling softly at her, he whispered, "Aye. Freely given." He leaned forward, kissing her softly and then groaning as the kiss deepened. His fingers dug into her back, holding her closer and then closer still, until they were breathless. Backing away, he dropped his head to kiss her neck and the racing pulse point there, before he scooted away, releasing her completely. "Enjoy your milk, Hett."

"Niall," she whimpered, desperate to be in his arms again.

A whisper-soft touch over her head and shoulder had her arching up and meeting his ardent gaze. "I love you, lass. Sleep well."

Watching him leave, she knew no amount of milk would calm her racing heart or roiling thoughts now.

CHAPTER 11

The next morning Hettie worked in the saloon, cleaning up from the evening before. She swept the floor before mopping it up and then moved to the small kitchen area in the back to finish washing any of the glasses that hadn't been cleaned after closing last night.

Elbow deep in soapy water, with her mind a million miles away as she considered her problems, she didn't hear him enter the room. Niall had always had that ability to move as quietly as a cat, when he wanted to. Or be as loud as a herd of buffalo. It used to amuse her but not today.

"Hett," he murmured, and she shrieked, dropping a glass with a dull *thud* in the sink.

"Don't sneak up on me," she snapped, as she glared at him over her shoulder. She scrubbed and scrubbed at the glass that was already clean, desperate for something to do with her hands. "What do you want?" Last night's quiet interlude seemed a million lifetimes' ago in the bright light of the morning.

"Hett," he murmured in that soft voice that always made her soften toward him.

Today it made her feel like she'd hurt him in some way. His green eyes shone with dread, as he held himself rigid, as though he were holding himself back from touching her. Or yanking her into his arms.

"What did you decide?"

Closing her eyes, she took a deep breath. Finally she dropped the glass into the water and dried her hands on a towel. "Nothing. I've decided nothing."

His shoulders straightened, and he smiled, while his eyes lit with joy. She watched, momentarily spellbound as he transformed, as though lit by the sun. "You're staying? With me?"

She shook her head, hating to see his brilliant delight dim. "No. I'm deciding. I ... I don't know what I'll do."

"You're staying, Hett, because you can't travel into the Territory. You don't have the money, and you can't go there alone."

Without thinking, she muttered, "Jacob gave me money." When Niall gripped her arms, she looked into his irate gaze and blanched at the fury she saw.

"What? The bastard gave you money? Like you're some common two-bit whore?"

Squirming and then swatting at him so he backed away, she panted with her anger and disappointment. "No! Not like that. Never like that. He'd never even think of me in that way. Or treat me like that." She glared at Niall, insinuating that he had. "He wanted to make sure I could travel to him. And have money for a hotel room in Helena. Before we wed." Her voice became weaker the more she spoke of Jacob's plan.

"*Jaysus*, you're really considering it." Niall backed away, until he bumped into an empty crate, stumbling until he reached out and braced himself with one arm on a wall. "After everything. After all we've shared, ... you're really thinking of leaving."

She jerked her head once, unable to speak. Her throat was tight, and all she wanted to do was cry. Why couldn't everything have been different between her and Niall before now?

"No," he rasped, marching toward her, his eyes glowing with a fervent determination. "I haven't lost you yet, Hett, and I refuse to lose you forever. Not to him. Not to any man. I love you. *You.* Not like a brother. Not like a bloody cousin. But like the woman I was always meant to be with. Like the way Da loves Mum or Finn, Winnie. With a madness I'll never recover from."

He shook his head, when she opened her mouth to argue with him. "Don't waste your breath, lass. You'll only make me angrier than I am now. And hurt me even more by ever doubtin' how much I love you."

He spun on his heels, storming away from her, leaving her breathless and stunned and desperate to believe herself worthy of his love.

Later that morning Henrietta had a few more chores she needed to do at the saloon, before heading to the café. She'd already watched the stagecoach trundle out of town, a few tears leaking out as she waved at Jacob. When Niall saw her swiping at her face, he'd glowered and stormed away. Now she was eager to finish her work here and be as far from Niall as she could for a little while.

"What's the matter, Hettie?" Winnie asked, as she followed her best friend upstairs. "I thought things were going well between you and Niall. Isn't he leaving you little love notes and presents?"

Hettie glared at Winnifred, as they moved into one of the four rooms upstairs that needed cleaning over the O'Rourke Saloon. "Not you too," Hettie muttered, as she entered the recently vacated room. She held up a hand and shook a finger at her best friend, who was happily married to Finn. "Don't act innocent. I know what everyone is attempting."

The teasing in Winnifred's gaze faded as she eyed her friend. "I'm sorry, Hettie. I thought you liked Niall. Although it didn't seem like you, teasing him with another man, when you really wanted Niall."

Stomping her foot, Hettie let out a groan and paced around the room, before slamming the door shut so they would be guaranteed a little more privacy. "Don't you understand that I do? I like Niall." Her brandy-colored eyes shone with regret and grief. "I adore him. I always have." Shaking her head, she sighed. "But it's hopeless. He only became interested in me after he learned about Jacob. He's not truly interested in me. Besides, I know how the family really thinks about me."

She sat on the rickety chair in the room, as Winnifred stared at her in dismay. "Can't you understand I want more than that? I want what you and Finn have." Her voice dropped to a near whisper. "Love."

Winnie plopped onto the edge of the bed and stared at Hettie in confusion. "I don't understand what you're saying, Hettie. What do you believe the family feels about you?"

"I see him talking with Lucien and Ardan and Seamus. I see how they quiet as I approach." Hettie lifted her chin. "I know they believe I'm not nearly good enough for Niall." She nodded, when Winnie blanched. "Don't try to deny it. I heard Declan say as much."

"Of course they go quiet. They want to respect you and *your* choice in another man." Winnie rubbed a hand through her hair. "If any of us had any sense, we'd shake you silly, so you'd see what you're throwing away by toying with Niall like this. And you must have misheard Declan. He'd never say that and mean it."

Hettie jumped up and glowered at her best friend. "I'm toying with *him*? I am?" She stomped her foot in aggravation. "He's the one toying with me! He's the one who can't stand the thought of anyone else liking me so that he must pretend to care for me."

"Oh, Hettie, that's so sad." Winnie shook her head mournfully and gazed at her with a profound sadness. "You can't see what's right in front of you. If you're not careful, you'll lose what you've always wanted."

Winnie rose, working with a silent efficiency, as Hettie stood rooted in place, Winnie's words ricocheting in her mind. Was Hettie blind, as Winnie implied? Was Hettie allowing fear to rule her emotions?

Uncertain, Hettie moved to another room, desperate to work alone today. However, even though she finished her work at the saloon in record time, and spent the day working in silence at the café, her mind never stopped coming up with ideas and possibilities. She thought she would go mad if she had one more vision of a perfect life with Niall. None of those visions were ever with Jacob. Why couldn't just one be with him? He was a nice man.

She remembered something she'd heard an O'Rourke brother mutter a few years ago. *Nice won't keep you warm at night.*

She shivered as she thought of those words. At the time, she hadn't understood what the brother had meant, but now she did. When she was with Jacob, everything was pleasant and lovely. With Niall, she felt alive. Like a candle lit her up inside.

And the kisses they'd shared only proved how much passion they had for each other. Why was she so afraid?

Setting down her paring knife, she took off her apron and muttered she needed a minute. Deirdre smiled at her, and Hettie raced from the café. She had to speak with Niall. She had to tell him that she'd realized she was a fool and that, of course, she trusted in his love. Of course she believed he loved her, as she did him.

She raced around to the front of the saloon, as the back was blocked by a delivery wagon, and stopped short. Niall was walking away, his stride purposeful. Following him, she was on the verge of calling out, when he turned in the direction of the Bordello. Madam Nora's establishment.

When he smiled and flirted with one of the Sirens, calling her sweetheart and speaking with her familiarly, Hettie froze.

"I've been waiting all day for you," the Siren called out.

"Patience is a virtue," he replied.

Hettie backed up in horror. When Niall leaned over, to whisper in the Siren's ear, Hettie thought she'd faint. Had he just kissed her? For everyone to see?

Niall didn't want *her*. He'd never wanted *her*. It was all a game. A game she was always meant to lose.

Spinning on her heel, she raced away, determined to get as far away from Niall, the O'Rourkes, and this town as soon as possible.

Niall sighed as he approached the Bordello. Madam Nora had summoned him, and he knew better than to ever ignore her summons. If all she needed was more whiskey, she would have sent a note. Irritated that he was being called away, just as the whiskey was being delivered, he paused at the Bordello threshold to wink and flirt with one of the Sirens, who used to work as a Temptress, before the O'Rourkes took over the running of the saloon.

"I've been waitin' all day for you," she called out, as she ran a hand down his arm.

Niall chuckled and winked at her, although he wondered if she called that out in a loud voice to attract attention and perhaps a customer. If it became known she'd enticed an O'Rourke, would she become the most coveted Siren? He decided to play along, and he smiled at her. "I bet you have, darlin'. All in good time." Then he called out in a loud voice, "Patience is a virtue." He tilted his head down to whisper in her ear, "And you'll be waitin' an eternity more. I've come to see the Madam." He looked toward the front door of the Bordello and frowned. "Where's the brute? He's always at the door."

The Siren shrugged and sashayed away. "He's around. He knows you won't cause trouble." She smiled and lowered her lashes. "Unless you want to."

Laughing, he shook his head, as he opened the door and closed it behind him. He'd been in the Bordello a few times to visit the Madam, generally with Seamus. He noted a few visitors, then headed toward the closed door at the rear of a long hallway and knocked.

Ezra jerked open the door and glowered at Niall, before stepping aside and letting him pass. Casting a glance at the huge man who ensured none of the Sirens were mistreated, Niall entered Madam Nora's office. Today she sat behind her desk, a few papers scattered on top. She wore a light-blue dress, and her eyes shone with disappointment, and she waved for him to sit.

"Madam?" Niall asked, as he plopped down in a chair. "Are you upset with the quality of whiskey?"

She huffed out a breath and leaned forward. "You are an *eejit*, as your da would say. Of course I'm not upset about the whiskey. If I were, I'd speak to your father." She sat back and held a pencil between her manicured fingers. "How can you let her go without a fight?"

Niall groaned and rose, pacing the area around the desk. "You have an opinion too?" He stared at her in disbelief. "Why can't everyone just let us figure this out on our own?"

"Because you're doing a terrible job of it," Nora snapped. "That man left today, and she cried over it. Where were you? Licking your wounds?" Nora threw down the pencil and stood, her hands on her desk. "You should have been there to haul her into your arms and to remind her that you were still here. That you were constant. That you would never leave her."

Niall stared at Nora like she was demented.

Or an Oracle.

"You know I'm right. You know you acted like a wounded little boy, all offended because the woman you love didn't just jump into your arms." She glared at him. "She's as confused and as scared as you are, Niall. And that man who left? He never made her feel that way. He made her feel wanted and seen and heard. Even if he's as interesting as a pile of manure."

Niall choked out a laugh and shook his head. "What would you know about him?"

"I talked with him for a little while. He enjoyed chatting with me, until he learned who I was." Her smile held a hint of mischief. "Then he looked dyspeptic. He acted as though my profession was catching."

Niall roared with laughter and shook his head. *"Eejit."* He sighed and gripped the back of the chair. "I don't know what more to do, Madam Nora. I've left her gifts with special notes. I've told her how I feel, more than once." He rubbed his forehead. "I can't make her love me."

Nora sat back in her chair and studied him. "Perhaps you are going about it all wrong. Perhaps the answer is to let her miss you. Let her go. Hopefully she'll have the sense to come back."

"And if she doesn't?" Niall whispered, hating that both Nora and Ardan were giving him the same distasteful advice.

"Then she wasn't yours to lose," Nora murmured, her gaze sorrowful. "As you just said, you can't make someone love you, Niall. No matter how much you might like to. It isn't possible."

Niall nodded. After a long moment of silence, he murmured his thanks and left, for there was nothing more to say. Madam Nora was correct. He couldn't force Hettie to love him, no matter how much he might want to.

~

Hettie raced to the livery and found Mr. Bailey sitting around, talking with the livery owner, Mr. Harrison. Other than Dunmore, he was the most respected stagecoach driver out of Fort Benton. She waited until they'd finished with one long-winded story, interrupting them before they could start on the next. "Mr. Bailey!" she called out. When he rose and approached her, she wrung her hands. "I know this is a busy time for you, but are you headed into the Territory soon?"

Bailey rubbed at his bald spot, before spitting out a stream of chewing tobacco. "Tomorrow. Why?"

"I must be on that stagecoach. I can sit on top or beside you. Please."

He stared at her. "Never knew anyone so desperate to escape the O'Rourkes. But then, word is, your love left this mornin'. I'll take you to Helena, miss. Don't you worry. And you'll be protected in the coach."

After giving an effusive thanks, she waved her arm at hearing they left at 7:00 a.m. sharp. She raced back to the café, knowing she'd been away too long. However, she needed some sort of plan to cling to, so she wouldn't focus on her heartache.

Just as she was about to enter the café, she thought she heard Niall call her name, but she ignored him. She couldn't face him. Not now. Instead she reentered the kitchen, pulled on her apron, washed her hands, and put her head down, as she focused on her work. She used another knife—anything but the special knife Niall had bought her—and got to work.

All afternoon and evening, she worked in silence, until finally it was time to go home. Just as she was about to depart for her bedroom and to silently pack her meager belongings, Ardan entered the kitchen. Belatedly Hettie noticed that Deirdre had already gone upstairs to be with Rory. "I hope you have a good evening, Ardan," she forced out, attempting to sound cheerful.

"Lass," Ardan said, with his mixture of compassion and authority, "sit." He motioned to one of the stools around the butcher block island and waited until she had complied. Then he sat beside her. "What happened this afternoon? You look like someone died."

"It's just been a trying day."

He placed a hand on her wrist to keep her from racing away, although he exerted no pressure. "No, Hettie, don't lie. Something happened. You weren't this upset when your man, Jacob, left this mornin'. Sure, you might have shed a few tears, but tonight you look like a woman who's lost all hope." He leaned forward and asked, "Should I go for Niall?"

"No!" she bellowed, before raising a hand to cover her mouth and to swallow down the sobs that wanted to burst forth. "No," she whispered, her eyes pleading with Ardan to leave her be.

"What did my brother do?"

"It doesn't matter. What matters is I learned I'd been correct to not believe in dreams. Dreams are for children. Dreams are for fools. Dreams are for ..." She broke off, as another sob threatened.

"Everyone, lass. They're for everyone. If you don't have dreams, life's not much worth livin'." He waited for her to say something, but, when she remained quiet, he spoke in a soft tone. "I know you think everything was easy for Deirdre and me. It wasn't. It was hard. She was scared. I was scared. But I realized I was more afraid of a life without her."

"He doesn't really want me, Ardan," she whispered, a tear leaking down her cheek. "I learned that today."

"Niall?" he asked, as though he had to clarify to ensure he knew which suitor she meant. When she nodded, he swore softly. "Don't be daft, lass. He's wanted you since you arrived. He was just too stupid to realize it."

Hettie let out a shaky breath and rose, leaning forward to kiss him on his cheek. "Thank you for always being like my big brother." She left, closing the rear door quietly behind her, so she wouldn't disturb Rory upstairs, leaving Ardan confused and feeling like she'd just said goodbye forever.

CHAPTER 12

The following morning Niall sat in the family kitchen, waiting for Hettie to come downstairs. He'd hoped to see her here last night. He'd left her a note and another gift on her pillow and had asked her to sit in the moonlight with him. To share a little time when the world was as quiet and as still as possible in the busy summer season.

Instead he'd waited for hours, staring at the doorway, as his hope dwindled. Why hadn't she come? Now again this morning he felt a horrible sense of déjà vu, as he watched and waited. Finally he rose and marched from the kitchen and up the stairs. If she was going to be cowardly, he'd force her from her room. She would listen to him, dammit!

Knocking on her door, he waited for her to tell him to go away. When she didn't say anything, he knocked louder, but there was no sound inside. Pushing the door open, he froze. The room was tidy, as though expecting a guest. The little things that made this Hettie's room were gone. The sketch he'd drawn her last year. The small rock collection from all the young O'Rourkes. The crooked twig they'd found on one of their rambles a few falls ago that they'd joked resembled their friendship.

Rushing to the closet, he jerked it open, to find the majority of her clothes missing. Spinning around, he found a note propped on the desk, and he snatched it up, flipping it open.

I'm sorry to leave like this. I never meant to sneak away, as though I'm ashamed. But I can't stay. Not now. Not after yesterday. Not after ...

Thank you for always believing in me and for giving me a home. Thank you for treating me so well all these years. I never felt like the hired help.

Hettie

Niall let out a roar, like a wild animal stuck in a trap, as he collapsed to his knees. As though from a long distance away, he heard the sound of chairs crashing and footsteps racing toward him, but he remained, kneeling and swaying in place, as he realized he'd lost her.

He'd lost Hettie.

She didn't love him enough.

Colleen was right. He wasn't lovable enough. He would never deserve the love of the woman of his dreams.

Hettie sat in the corner of the stagecoach, clutching her coat to her, even though it was at least ten degrees hotter inside the stifling stagecoach than it was outside. She prayed they'd arrive at the next stop soon, so she could get out and stretch her legs. Being crammed inside with so many pungent men was a special kind of torture.

Now that she had left Fort Benton, doubts bloomed. Should she have confronted Niall, rather than run away? Should she have met him downstairs, as he had wanted last night, and thrown the chocolate in his face and torn up his note as she yelled at him?

With a sigh, she held her coat closer, knowing that she was most likely melting the chocolate, which she brought with her, the chocolate that he'd left on her pillow last night. She didn't care if she crumpled the note. It would survive. Besides, she had it memorized.

Hettie, my love,

You are sweeter than any chocolate, but I want to spoil you.

Meet me in the kitchen, when the world is quiet, so we can dance in the moonlight together.

I long to hold you in my arms and to have time with you, when no words suffice for all we feel.

Niall

A tear coursed down her cheek. "Why?" she whispered to herself. *Why* she asked herself, when a man looked at her with interest. After flirting with the Siren yesterday as he entered the Bordello, why would Niall continue with his farce of being interested in her? He had to know she would find out about his visit there. People like Janet Davies were only too delighted to report on the goings-on in the O'Rourke family in the hopes of sowing discord. Or did he think that Hettie would be willing to share him?

She wanted to scream. She would never share him. Not with how she felt. A murderous rage and then a deep sorrow filled her at the thought of Niall with anyone but her, and she resented that he'd forced her to witness his flirtation, even unwittingly. Now she understood how he'd felt the past week, as she'd gone out to supper with Jacob.

Huffing out a sigh, Hettie looked out the window at the never-ending burned brown prairie land. The rolling hills and bluffs were in the distance, but she'd never seen such an uninspiring landscape. She should have listened in more when Dunmore talked about his trips through the Territory, rather than whispered silly jokes and stories to Niall.

Niall. Just thinking his name evoked pain. When would she ever overcome her love for him and his betrayal?

Seamus was the first in the room, and he fell to the floor by his son. He ignored the note in Niall's hand and gripped Niall's shoulders. "Lad, what's happened?"

"She left." Niall spoke, as though he were in a trance, and held out the slip of paper. He fell backward, so he leaned against the edge of her bed, while he watched his da read the note. "I don't know what she meant about yesterday. Unless she realized how much she missed ... *him*." His voice was laced with venom, as he referred to Jacob Morrissey.

Mary gasped in dismay and snatched the letter from Seamus, reading it before passing it on. She knelt beside Niall. "No, it can't be that, my little love."

More footsteps pounded up the stairs, the room now full of so many people. Finally Ardan poked his head inside. He pushed the pack out and shut the door, so it was only him and his parents with Niall. "I just heard from Mr. Harrison, who came in for breakfast." His gaze was sorrowful as he stared at Niall. "Hettie left this mornin'?"

"Aye," Seamus said, "but we don't know why."

Sighing, Ardan ran a hand over his face. "I had the oddest conversation with her last night. She said she'd realized she was stupid to dream. And then 'twas like she was wishin' me goodbye forever, but that made no sense." He paused, as he gazed into his brother's desolate eyes. "Until now."

"What could have happened yesterday?" Mary demanded. "She wasn't enamored of that man, no matter what she says." She squeezed Niall's shoulder. "Hettie loves Niall."

Niall focused on his mum using the present tense, although he felt like he had such little reason for hope. "Thanks, Mum," he whispered. Gazing at his brother, he whispered, "Isn't this what you said? I have to let her go and see if she returns?"

Ardan crouched down and met his wounded gaze with one filled with compassion. "I'd hoped it would be something less drastic, like letting her go a week or so without seein' you. Not somethin' like this."

"Aye," Seamus murmured. "She's a woman alone in the Territory. Anythin' could happen to her."

"Do I chase after her?" Niall asked in a low voice, lacking all enthusiasm.

"Not today, lad, not today."

Niall didn't voice what they all knew: there was no other stagecoach in town that could drive him anywhere, and they didn't know how long until there would be one.

Seamus heaved Niall up. "Today, bury yourself in work. An' try not to start any fights." He squeezed his son's shoulders, as he shared a mournful glance with his wife, wishing there were something more he could do to ease his son's heartache.

Three days later Hettie emerged from her hotel in Helena, a decent establishment, but not one that would run through all her meager funds quickly. She continued to search for Jacob, desperate to find him in this sea of people she didn't know. Desperate to find anyone she knew so she wouldn't feel so alone.

After living in Fort Benton for the past four years, she'd forgotten what it was like to live in a large town or city. Although not large in comparison to a city like Saint Louis, it felt like Helena teemed with people, businesses, and wagons carting goods everywhere. On her first day in town, she was almost run over twice, and she now hated attempting to cross the main road in town. So much larger than Fort Benton, Helena overwhelmed Hettie, and she had trouble sleeping at night, as an ever-growing onslaught of her fears for her future filled her mind.

Her thoughts circled on a never-ending loop, keeping her from sleeping well. Would she be happy? Would she forget Niall? Would she find Jacob in time? What would happen to her if she didn't? Every morning she woke up more tired than when she went to sleep, determined to forge a successful future and yet fearful she'd made a mistake but with no way to rectify it.

Deep inside, she understood her desperation. If she didn't find Jacob soon, she didn't know what she'd have to do. She pushed that thought out of her mind again, as she couldn't bear to contemplate a future alone and unsupported by any friends. She refused to envision what she might be forced to do if ... With a sigh, she ran a hand over her skirt and slipped from her hotel room, determined that today would be the day she was successful with her search. Today her future would truly begin.

As she descended the stairs, she continued to think about the difference between her arrival in Helena and in Fort Benton. It hadn't taken her more than five minutes in Helena to understand her immense fortune in meeting the O'Rourkes and being adopted into their clan. She was the fool for ever doubting her place among them.

Today she entered the restaurant attached to the hotel for her noontime meal, longing for a home-cooked O'Rourke meal or for a scrumptious meal prepared by Deirdre. Instead Hettie had to suffer through another overcooked, underflavored meal, playing the game of "guess what meat this is covered in a mound of gravy." Soon she'd depart for another day of searching for Jacob and evading the leering gazes and advances of unsavory men.

She pushed the food around on her plate, studiously avoiding the glances of the many men in the dining room. She'd learned that, if she smiled or appeared interested, she'd have a meal companion who would be hard to shake loose. Instead she attempted to appear vapid and kept her head down.

At the commotion at the dining room door, her heart leaped for a moment, imagining that Niall had tracked her down. Her heart landed with a *thud* when she saw Jacob pushing his way toward her, with a delighted smile. In that instant, any doubt she'd had about her decision immediately cleared, and she knew she'd been a fool.

Now she was a fool stuck in Helena, with no way to return to Fort Benton to confront the man she loved.

"Miss Foyle!" he exclaimed, as he grabbed her free hand and kissed it, sitting across from her before she could even invite him to join her. "I can't believe you're already here."

Feigning joy, she smiled back. "I'm here!" she parroted, feeling like the village idiot. If Niall were beside her, he'd make a silly remark, and they'd burst into laughter. Instead Jacob puffed up and seemed even prouder. Somehow he was interpreting her hasty arrival as a reflection of her overwhelming desire to marry him. She bit her lip, as she realized that was a rational reaction on his part.

Her fingernails bit into the soft flesh of her palms, as she wished Niall sat across from her. Or that she were brave enough to admit she'd made a mistake and to ask Jacob for the fare to return home. For Fort Benton was home. Instead she smiled at Jacob, acting how she thought he wanted her to act.

"Don't worry. I'll speak to the preacher, and we'll wed within a few days. I've found a house, and it's beautiful."

Hettie nodded, unable to conceal the panic in her gaze. "It's all so soon."

Looking around the room at the curious stares of the other men, he dropped his voice and murmured, "What did you expect? This is how it has to be."

"Of course," Hettie murmured, gasping when he reached below the table and grabbed her hand. He lifted it so it was on top of the table and slid a ring on her finger. She stammered, "I don't think ... That's to say ... That's not ..."

"Of course it's proper. And it will prevent anyone from getting the wrong idea." He frowned, as he gazed down at the simple ring, with the sapphire chip in it. "It's only slightly too big. I'll have it sized for you soon."

"Jacob," she whispered, "I thought I'd have my month to figure things out." When he looked at her with pity, she blanched and forced a laugh. "How silly of me. I never expected you'd be so ... keen on marrying so soon." He'd professed he would never love her, so why the rush? They shared no passion, as she'd felt little more for him than friendship when they'd kissed. Nothing like the overwhelming desire with ... Closing her eyes, she pushed away those thoughts about Niall. She had to stop thinking about him. Focusing on Jacob again, she attempted a smile.

Staring at her, he nodded, kissing her hand again. "Of course I'm keen on marrying you. Only a fool wouldn't be."

She frowned, as it sounded like a criticism of Niall, but how would he know of Niall? All she wanted to do was return to her room and hide for the next decade, but she knew that wasn't possible. Setting aside her napkin, she placed her hands in her lap.

He rose, holding his hand out for hers, and slipped it through his arm. "Let's walk around Helena. It's a fine town and growing every day." He preened, as men eyed him with envy to have Hettie on his arm.

She wished she felt as proud to be on his arm. He was handsome and kind but not Niall. Her mind flashed back to Niall with the Siren, and she wanted to weep. Why had he betrayed her? She blinked rapidly, so she wouldn't cry, and focused on Jacob and his talk about the number of new businesses opening each year and the dream of train travel to the Territory someday soon.

The main street was lined with brothels, hotels, saloons, and restaurants. Barber shops, laundries, and other stores vied for space but were overshadowed by their more flamboyant neighbors. The main street was much larger than Fort Benton's, but, in many ways, it was similar. Too many men loitered around with too little to do, as they told tales about fictitious exploits.

Squeezing her arm, he murmured in her ear, "I don't want you wandering town on your own. This is a wild place."

"Even after we're married?"

"Especially then. You'll have our home to decorate, and soon you'll meet other women you can pay calls on. Respectable women." He smiled down at her. "We can go on walks together. You'll be my responsibility when we marry, Hettie, and I can't have anything happen to you."

"I'm not her, Jacob," she protested. "The same thing won't happen again."

"You can't know that. I will protect you." His blue eyes shone with a touch of derision, as he said, "I know you wandered freely in Fort Benton, but you should never have been allowed to walk without an escort. The O'Rourkes were foolish to have risked your safety."

Hettie bristled at his criticism of the O'Rourkes but bit back her retort. She swallowed, suddenly realizing how much the loss of his first wife had affected him and how his fears might make him irrational. After the freedoms she'd had in Fort Benton, and, conversely, the constant company from the various members of the O'Rourke family, she feared she'd go mad if she had to live her life locked away alone in a home, no matter how fine it was.

When she sensed him staring down at her, she nodded and feigned a smile, wondering if she'd just consigned herself to a life in a gilded cage.

CHAPTER 13

Niall sat on a stool in the saloon, long after closing time. The floors were swept, glasses washed, and tables wiped down. He had no reason to be here, but he had no desire to go home. He wouldn't run into Hettie in the kitchen. He wouldn't hear her softly singing to herself in her room. He wouldn't smile at her, as they shared a private joke at breakfast.

She was gone, and he doubted she'd return.

He remembered Ardan and Finn, racing after Deirdre and Winnie. He'd always thought that romantic and just what you did when the woman you loved left.

When you thought you'd die if she wasn't with you.

Instead he sat.

He had no desire to chase after her, even if he could. Dunmore and Bailey were both out of town, and Niall had no idea when they'd be back. Besides, Hettie didn't want him to follow her. She'd left without even having the decency to say goodbye.

That was what hurt the worst. She'd left a damn note. She'd snuck away, like a thief in the night. Instead of stealing the family silver, if they had had any, she'd stolen his heart, and he didn't know how he'd survive.

With a groan, he rested his head on his crossed arms, wishing he could think about anything other than Hettie. But he couldn't. She filled his mind, and the memories played of all the time they'd had together, over and over again.

He wished all he felt was bitterness or anger. That he could cling to the hurt. Instead a chasm of regret filled him, and he knew it would never fully heal. If he'd not been a fool. If he'd only realized sooner how much she meant to him. If he'd only been braver.

You'll see. No woman will ever love or want you.

He shivered as his mother's words slithered through his mind, and he pushed them away. He wished they were false. He wished they had no power over him.

But he knew wishes were pointless.

If wishes were worth anything, Hettie would be here. Dreaming of him, not of some other man, who would never love her like he did.

Nearly a week later, Hettie was a bundle of nerves. She'd managed to postpone the wedding a few days, but she knew she couldn't escape the choices she'd made.

Tomorrow she'd marry Jacob. Tomorrow she'd be separated from Niall forever. Holding a dress to her chest, she closed her eyes, as she battled abject terror. Jacob was a good man. He was kind and attentive and genuinely concerned for her welfare. When she was with him, she felt like he could become a wonderful friend.

Yet he never made her laugh so hard that her stomach hurt, with tears racing down her cheeks. He never had a secret smile, just for her, that showed her how much he adored her. He never looked at her with a simmering passion in his gaze. Now that she was away from Niall, she understood what that look meant. It was a look all O'Rourke men had, when they gazed at their women. She hadn't expected to see it from Niall and had mistrusted it.

Why had she mistrusted Niall? Why couldn't she believe he would care for her? Why had she believed the horrible words from a woman like Mrs. Davies over what Niall said? Hettie ducked her head in shame, as she wished she'd behaved with the confidence she acted like she had, but was all for show.

Instead, inside she was a terrified ten-year-old, determined to be seen as worthy and lovable and not be abandoned again. If the O'Rourkes—Niall—knew the truth, no one would truly want her. No one would truly love her.

Rather than be abandoned, she'd done the abandoning.

Her breath whooshed out of her at that realization, and she collapsed onto one of the chairs, the dress crumpled on her lap, as she gazed at her messy room. She was packing up, something that should take fifteen minutes but was taking hours. She was dithering.

Her mind swirled with the questions she could not answer. Was she wrong to leave Fort Benton? Did Niall truly betray her with that Siren? Was it always hopeless between them?

She let out a sigh and pinched the bridge of her nose. "Naive fool," she hissed at herself. "You know what you saw. Quit trying to find a way so your heart isn't broken." She fought tears because, in the end, it didn't matter. She couldn't return to Niall anyway.

Tomorrow she would marry, and she would be happy, even if it killed her.

Hettie froze at the insistent *thump* on her hotel room door. It wasn't the polite tapping from Jacob. She held her breath, and the thumping began again.

"Hettie?" a man called out. A deep gravelly voice, which she recognized.

Rushing to the door, she yanked it open and gazed into the confused eyes of Dunmore, his long hair pulled back and his hat in one hand. He looked like he needed a wash and a change of clothes, and fatigue clung to him. She'd never been so delighted to see anyone in her life. "What are you doing here?"

"I was going to ask you that question, lass." He made a motion, and she nodded. After entering the room and closing the door, he peered down at her. "Helena, lass? You couldn't have found a better place?"

"Is there one in the Territory?" she asked, with her head tilted up and a grimace on her face. Yet she wanted to throw herself into his arms and beg him to take her back to Fort Benton, but she knew she had no right. She had no money to pay him. Besides, she'd run away. She'd betrayed the O'Rourkes.

Sighing, he set his hat on a clear spot on her bureau and sat on one of the two chairs in the room. "All right. Let's hear it." He stared at her like he had all day and wasn't in need of a meal and a trip to the bathhouse. "Bailey told me that he'd delivered you here, or I wouldn't have detoured back on my way home." He nodded, meeting her wide-eyed gaze. "Couldn't return home without tryin' to find you."

"You sought me out?" At his nod, she collapsed onto a pile of clothes on her bed. "Why?"

"You're one of us, lass." He frowned when his simple comment made her hold a hand to her mouth, as she battled a sob. "What's goin' on?"

"I … I'm getting married tomorrow." Her voice hitched on the word *married*.

"The hell—" Dunmore broke off what he would have said but glowered at her. "No, you ain't. Try again."

"I left Fort Benton." When he stared at her with his implacable stare, as though that were obvious because they were sitting in a hotel room in Helena, she crumbled forward, and, between sobs and wails, the whole story poured forth. Her love for Niall. Her mistrust of his constancy. Her realization that she'd been a fool, after seeing him flirt with a Siren. She fell silent when Dunmore held up a hand.

"You ran when you saw him with a Siren?" At her nod, he rubbed at his head. "Was he in a compromisin' position?"

She furrowed her brows and then flushed beet red. "Of course not! They were standing at the doorway. He winked at her and flirted with her. She said she'd been waiting all day for him, and he didn't contradict her. He leaned forward, and I think he might have kissed her cheek."

Groaning, Dunmore's head fell forward, until it rested on his hands, bracketed on his knees. "Ah, lass, that was just Trudy, flirtin' like she does with every man who comes into the Bordello. Niall always treats her with courtesy because she used to be a Temptress, and Bell was a beast to her."

"Trudy?" Hettie whispered. "I don't remember her."

"Aye, well, now you know who she is. The worst flirt to ever be a Siren. She can't help herself, and Seamus has instilled it in all his lads to always be courteous, even when they're not interested." He tilted his head to stare at her. "Why didn't you yell at him and call him names? Why run from him?"

She shrugged, a tear leaking out.

"Well, now you'll have to eat crow, lass."

"How?" she wailed. "I'm getting married tomorrow!"

He grinned at her. "Are you?" He rose and held out his hand. "Come. Dry your face, and we'll figure out what to do. Lucky for you, the passenger seat beside me is empty for my return trip tomorrow, although we'll have to find you a good-size bonnet. Wouldn't do to have you turn up looking like a ripe tomato."

Niall stared at the saloon door again, wishing Hettie was walking through it with Winnie. Instead Winnie and Maggie chattered away, as they entered to head upstairs to clean and tidy things. A black cloud of rage enveloped Niall, and he strode over to his brother's wife and Hettie's best friend, towering over her. He rasped, "Did you know?"

Winnie gaped at him, wide-eyed, and shook her head. Before she'd married Finn, she'd been filled with bravado, but, ever since they'd married, and she'd fully reconciled with all the O'Rourkes, her true nature had shone through. Winnie had been nothing but kind and funny and sweet.

"Don't lie to me, Winnie!"

She paled as he roared at her and shook her head again. "I'm not, Niall. I had no idea." Her eyes filled. "How do you think I felt when my best friend left with no word to me?" A tear dripped down her cheek, and she sniffled.

Just as quickly as the rage came upon him, it faded, and he took a step back, ashamed at his actions. "Winnie, I'm sorry. I'm …" He closed his eyes and missed her pitying look.

"Missing her," she whispered.

What more she might have said was broken off, when Niall was roughly shoved aside by Finn, who'd burst into the saloon. He tugged Winnie into his arms and glared daggers at his brother. "I'll kill you for upsetting her," he whispered, before focusing on his wife. "Are you all right, little love?"

She nodded, resting her head against Finn's shoulder. "Don't fret, darling. He's missing Hettie and needing someone to be angry with."

Niall flushed, as he knew his older brother wouldn't let this end with an apology. If Niall were really unlucky, Da would find out, and then there would be hell to pay. "Finn—"

"Don't even bother." Finn wrapped an arm around Winnie's shoulders and walked her upstairs, saying soothing things to her the entire time.

Rubbing a hand over his face, Niall turned for the bar, a hitch in his step when he saw Lucien watching him with frank disappointment. "I said I was sorry," Niall snapped, picking up a towel and slapping it against the edge of the wooden bar.

Niall let out a long breath at the pronounced silence coming from his brother and then took another deep breath. This simmering rage he felt wasn't going away. It was growing and growing, and he didn't know what to do with it.

"Talk to Da," Lucien urged. "He knows what it is to lose the woman he loves. He lost Mum for too long."

Closing his eyes, Niall silently acknowledged his brother was right. Niall had to talk to someone, and his da would listen. Da would still love Niall, no matter what he said or did.

"Go," Lucien urged. "We're not too busy yet, and the lads are here." He grinned, as he saw Bryan and Henri attempting to perfect their poker game at the opposite end of the bar. They had so many tells that they would be fleeced the minute they sat down for a game with real card players, but they enjoyed playing each other.

Niall nodded and left out the back door. After the short walk to the warehouse, he poked his head into his da's office, smiling when he saw his da steadily working through a pile of papers. Although he claimed to hate paperwork, he always did everything he needed to ensure the businesses thrived.

"Da," Niall whispered. When Seamus looked up at him and smiled, Niall felt like weeping. "I don't know what to do." After shutting the door behind him, Niall collapsed in the chair across from his da and waited for Seamus to speak.

"Do you want to go after her?"

Niall stilled. His da always went straight to the heart of the matter. "She doesn't want me, Da. She wants him." His shoulders stooped, he hung his head. "I think that's what hurts the most." His green eyes shone with the agony of Hettie's rejection. "She didn't want me."

"Ah, lad," Seamus murmured as he rose, stilling when Finn burst into the room, shouting, "Where is he?"

Niall stood, barely rising before Finn attacked him, knocking him to the ground. Grunting, Niall rolled, and soon he and Finn were pushing and punching, kicking and hitting each other as best they could. Elbows, fists, and knees connected, earning grunts and moans.

Finn bashed Niall's head with his elbow, and Niall saw stars a second, before he dodged another blow. Then, just as suddenly, Finn was gone. Niall shook his aching head and saw Kevin and Da yanking Finn away, holding him back, as he tried to lunge for Niall yet again, like a rabid dog.

"I said I was sorry. Dammit, Finn," Niall hissed, as he touched his head and came away with a smear of blood. "I already felt like a jackass before you stormed into the saloon. You raging around like a lunatic doesn't help."

"You made Winn cry," Finn hissed in a low voice, his blue eyes shining with an unholy anger.

"So did you!" Niall snapped, hopping up to his feet, battling dizziness and the urge to throw up. *Wow*, Niall marveled, *Finn fought dirty. But then I'd fight dirty too, if someone made Hettie cry.* He hated thinking he'd been the one to make her sad or to make her cry. Why else would she have left? He closed his eyes for a moment and spoke in a soft voice, "I'm sorry, Finn. I apologized to Winnie. I would have said more, but you interrupted us."

Kevin spoke up in a gentle but authoritative voice that only an older brother had. "We've all been fools in love, Finn. And Niall didn't know. He would never have acted like he did if he understood."

"Understood what?" Niall asked, still woozy on his feet, his hands on his hips, as he stared at his family, suddenly feeling like an outsider, as they all knew a secret he didn't. That had never happened before, and he hated feeling like this.

"Winn's expecting another baby," Finn said, unable to hide a proud grin. "She's exhausted and weepy, missing Hettie enough without you making her feel bad."

Now Niall felt about two inches tall for making his pregnant sister-in-law cry. "Finn." He shook his head and swore softly, as regret overwhelmed him. He righted the overturned chair and collapsed onto it, feeling like an outcast in his own family. Everyone was happy but him. Everyone had a future they looked forward to. He'd be the bachelor uncle they all whispered about. The man so foolish that he'd lost the woman he loved.

Seamus motioned for everyone to leave, and soon Niall was alone again with his father. The door *click*ed shut, and Niall heard the soft rumble of his brothers' voices, as they departed from the warehouse. Now the silence in his da's office was overwhelming.

He sat with a ducked head, dreading seeing the disapproval in his da's gaze. "I messed up, Da."

Seamus sat beside him, and Niall saw him cross his ankles. Da didn't speak, and Niall finally looked up. At the tender look in his da's eyes, he wanted to weep. "*Da.*"

Nodding, Seamus remained quiet.

"I don't know what to do," Niall blurted out. "I'm angry and miserable, and I want to scream and make everyone feel as awful as I do." He leaned forward with a groan. "And I'm so ashamed. I'm the one who messed up."

"Why do you say that?" Seamus murmured.

Niall rubbed at his eyes, swiping away the moisture that wanted to leak out. "She wouldn't have run if I'd convinced her that I was sincere. She wouldn't have run if I'd shown her how much I loved her. She wouldn't have run if …" He broke off what he would have said, hanging his head even lower.

"If you were a better man?" Seamus asked, waiting until Niall raised his head enough to meet his gaze. "If you were lovable enough?" His blue eyes blazed with a deep intensity that wasn't rage but bordered on it. "You are infinitely lovable, my boy. You are precious as you are."

He squeezed his son's shoulder, smiling softly. "Your mother lied, but I can't convince you of that. You must come to believe it on your own."

Niall gave up his battle on holding back his tears, and a steady stream coursed down his cheeks. "What should I do, Da? I love her, but I didn't go after her. What does that say about me?"

Seamus stared at a spot over Niall's shoulder for a moment and shook his head. "Only you can decide what to do, and it shows no bearing on your love for her, Niall." He squeezed his son's shoulder again. "When you need to rage, pummel a brother or yell at me, all right?"

Niall nodded. Although nothing had been decided or improved by talking to his da, Niall felt better. His da's quiet, constant love always eased his torment.

"Might I ask one question?" Seamus murmured, and Niall focused on his da. "As you try to determine what it is you want to do, why is it you can believe your mother's lies with such ease, while denying my truth?"

"What?"

"I love you, Niall. I'm proud of you. I near burst with joy at the sight of you. You're worthy of my love and esteem." He paused, frowning when he saw the doubt creep into his son's eyes. "Yet you believe in her spiteful and petty lies more than in me and what I've shown you to be true every moment since you were born."

Niall sat, dumbfounded, as he gazed at his father. "Da, … I …"

Seamus patted his leg. "Aye, 'tis a lot to take in. Think about it, son." He slipped from the room, gifting Niall with a quiet place to consider everything that had happened that day.

~

Taking a deep breath, Hettie firmed her shoulders and forced herself to walk up the church steps, with Dunmore a few steps behind her. He said that he'd let her say her piece to Jacob but that he wasn't leaving her alone to face an angry, disappointed man. Although Hettie wanted to insist she could break off her engagement without a witness, she was relieved she wouldn't be alone.

Hettie pushed open the church door, holding her breath at the resounding quiet inside. The faint hint of incense scented the air, and the light was a bit hazy when entering the high windows. Her bootheels clicked and echoed off the pine floor, heralding her arrival, and she wished she could have entered more quietly.

The minute Jacob saw her, Hettie knew he understood something was wrong. She wasn't wearing wedding finery, but a traveling dress with sturdy boots. She paused halfway down the aisle, not wishing to approach the altar. "Jacob," she whispered, her hands knitted together so she wouldn't wring them. She wanted him to have no doubt about her decision, but she remained nervous about talking with him and disappointing him. "I'm returning to Fort Benton today."

He approached her, dressed in his finest black suit with a gray waistcoat and a blazingly white shirt and collar. His blue eyes, their brightness enhanced by his formal attire, shone with disbelief. Gripping her arm, he shook his head, his gaze pleading with her. "No, my darling Hettie, you're not. You're marrying me, and we're starting our life together. Today." He motioned for her to follow him up the aisle to the altar, and she backed up a step.

"No, Jacob. Listen to me. I'm sorry. I was wrong. I was stupid and wrong. I shouldn't have come. I ... I love someone else." She winced as she saw him jerk at her words, the hopeful gleam in his eyes fading to distrust and disbelief.

Jacob looked over her shoulder at Dunmore, loitering in the shadows, and shook his head. "No, I think you're being coerced. I think you have no choice." He lowered his voice. "Be brave, Hettie. Live a life free of that family. With me."

A tear leaked out. "I'm so sorry for hurting you. You're a wonderful man." A smile burst forth. "But I'm not being coerced. I'm choosing to return. And I couldn't be happier."

Dunmore cleared his throat, and Hettie knew it was time for her to leave. They needed to start on their way, and there was no reason to prolong this moment. She grabbed Jacob's hand and pressed a small bag into it. "This should cover the expense of my journey here. My hotel room has been paid for. And my ring. It's in the bag, too."

His fist closed around the bag, and he backed up a step. "As you desire, go then." He paused a long moment, as his blue eyes shone with regret. "I wish you happy, Henrietta."

Rising on her toes, she kissed his cheek, whispering, "As I do for you."

She spun, racing away, eager to start the journey home.

Turning his face up to the sun, Niall tried to find the peace that had eluded him ever since Hettie had left. Neither Dunmore nor Bailey had returned since Hettie had stolen away.

Stolen away.

What an apt way of describing how he felt. She'd stolen away with his heart, and he didn't know when he'd ever recover. Now, on top of missing Hettie with a bone-deep ache, he had to contend with his brother's rage and his sister-in-law's sorrow.

How had Niall managed to mess up everything so profoundly?

As he battled to push down the ever-present rage that Hettie had left with no explanation, he thought about his conversation with Da. Niall had never doubted his da's love, the constancy of his da's devotion to family and to him. Why then had he found it easier to believe his mother's words than his father's actions?

Niall stared at the creek that was drying up, like the hope in his heart for Hettie's return, with an aching clarity. He needed to have faith in the actions of those around him, not their words.

Hettie had shown him how she truly felt when she ran from him. No matter how hard it was to accept that truth, Niall had to find a way to find peace with her choices.

Letting out a shaky breath, he tried to as easily let go of the painful hold his mother's words still had over him. With time, he hoped he'd have more faith in those who'd always showed him their love, than in the one who'd only ever treated him with disdain.

Hettie tilted her head up to the sun on one of the few stops they'd take on their journey back to Fort Benton. She smiled as she imagined sharing many moments like this with Niall in the future. In her mind, she envisioned walking with him, hand in hand, as they strolled around town and on the trails near town, laughing, talking, and stealing kisses.

She pushed aside her panic that he would no longer want her, after she'd acted like a coward and left. Hopefully his love was stronger than his anger, and he'd find a way to forgive her.

Letting out a shaky breath, she knew she'd have to find a way to explain to him why she'd acted as she had. His speaking with the Siren wasn't the only reason. Her fragile confidence after her abandonment as a child had caused her to have little faith in the constancy of those who professed their love and devotion.

Opening her eyes, she looked around her. The sun was still high in the sky, and they had hours to go before they'd stop again to change the horses. She tightened the strings of her bonnet, thankful Dunmore had charmed a woman in Helena into selling him this garment, as it helped protect her from the unremitting heat. Looking over the prairie, she enjoyed even the burnished gold grass as it waved in the wind, undulating gently. The only scar on the pristine landscape was the wagon rut carved in the ground.

Nearby, men loitered and chatted as they moaned, groaned, and stretched, thankful for a few moments out of the stagecoach. None approached her, and she was thankful they gave her a wide berth. It was as though she were on a foreign land, and none were willing to visit her. Rather than feeling upset, she was relieved. No man on this trip interested her.

Closing her eyes again, she enjoyed the feel of the wind and the sun and imagined hearing Niall's soft voice. That would be heaven.

"Lass," Dunmore called out in his raspy voice, "you have about five more minutes before we start out again."

She opened her eyes and met his patient gaze. All throughout the journey back, she'd sat beside him, with him pointing out landmarks, answering questions, and remaining quiet when he sensed she was lost to her own thoughts. He was, she realized, the ideal older brother.

"Thank you," she whispered, suddenly feeling shy and embarrassed.

"What's the matter, Hettie?" He strode to her, his long hair flowing over his shoulders, as his eyes blazed with concern. He was a tall, lean man, with a latent strength, and few were willing to take him on in a fight. "Who bothered you?" Dunmore had made it clear from the first moment of this journey that Hettie was under his protection and that any man who pestered her would be flung into the wilds of the Territory to rot.

"No one," she whispered. "I'm thinking you're an ideal older brother, and I'm so lucky."

The anger faded, replaced by embarrassment as he flushed. "Well, can't let the O'Rourkes have all the best honorary titles," he teased. "Besides, my Maggie adores you, and Lorcan considers you his aunt."

She paled. "I fear he won't want me back."

Dunmore shrugged, knowing she was referring to Niall and not his two-year-old son. "Ah, he might be angry, which is his right. He might be hesitant, which is natural. But he ain't no fool." He grinned at her. "None of the O'Rourkes are when it comes to love. He'll want you back and will celebrate your return. Never doubt that, lass."

He turned from her and let out a loud whistle, so the men

wandering near the stagecoach returned and boarded again. "Come. Let me heave you up."

Hettie giggled, as that had become one of their jokes. She'd had trouble crawling up to the stagecoach seat in her heavy skirts, and Dunmore had given up with the niceties, heaving her up so she felt like she was flying through the air. Now he saved her the embarrassment of trying and failing to climb up and simply hefted her there.

Walking back to the stagecoach with an eager skip in her step, Hettie couldn't wait to continue their journey. Every moment on the stagecoach, bumping along in uncomfortable misery, was one less moment away from Niall.

CHAPTER 14

Niall worked by rote in the saloon. He filled glasses, made change, smiled when he thought it was appropriate, but heard very little of what occurred right around him. Over a week had passed, and all he could think was *She left. She left. She left.* It was a never-ending thought in his mind, and he wondered if he'd ever be free of it.

He tried not to resent his family, but it was hard. They were loving and understanding, but, if he heard one more conversation end abruptly at his arrival, he thought he'd scream. If he saw one more pitying look, he worried he'd toss a customer out a window. If he heard Bryan say, "She'll be back" in his naive, confident young voice one more time, Niall was going to throw himself in the Missouri and happily drown.

Damn them all. They had no idea what this was like. He wished he'd run after her. Pride be hanged. He wished he'd found some way to never have hurt her, although his anger at her grew every day because she hadn't confronted him. She'd run instead.

With a sigh, he attempted to bite back a snarl when Lucien approached him, but Niall knew he had failed when Luc stared at him with mild disapproval. "Da wants you. In his office. Now."

Niall looked around the saloon, bustling with customers. "I can't leave you."

"No argument. Da wanted you there five minutes ago, Niall."

Groaning, Niall rubbed at his forehead and yanked off his apron before slamming out the back door. Thank God for Bryan and Henri. They were working harder than Lucien and Niall had expected, but they were doing a wonderful job. And, with how surly Niall had been, they were becoming the favorite O'Rourkes with their customers, especially Bryan, with his penchant for storytelling.

Storming into the warehouse, he barely spared a glance for Oran and Kevin, although Niall's glare intensified at their gleeful looks. How could they find his misery entertaining? Pushing open Da's door, he was already speaking. "Da, I'm busy. Can't this wait 'til tonight? Nothin's more important than helpin' Luc. An' tryin' to forget."

Seamus lifted an eyebrow and eyed him thoughtfully. "Nothing?"

The door swung shut behind Niall, and he spun around, falling back a step at the sight of Hettie. "Sweet *Jaysus*, I'm seein' ghosts now. I've gone mad."

She laughed and held a hand to her mouth, as she swallowed a sob. "You're not dreaming, Niall. I'm here. I came back."

His eyes closed for the briefest of moments, as the sweet sound of her soft voice washed over him. Opening his eyes again, his hungry gaze roved over her, searching for signs that she was well. Unharmed. At the joy and yet trepidation in her eyes, as though she were delighted at seeing him again, he took a small step toward her.

"You ran from me. You ran to him." His green eyes shone with pain. He clenched and unclenched his hands, as all he wanted to do was haul her into his arms and kiss her until they couldn't remember their names. Kiss her until she admitted she loved him too. Trusted him. Would take a chance on him.

He heard his da slip from the room, and Niall was alone with Hettie. This time, it was different from every other time they'd been together. This time, it meant so much more. "Hettie?"

Her name. Such a simple word—yet laced with so much hope and doubt and fear.

"I'm sorry," she whispered. "I was afraid, and I ran. I missed you every second. I ..." She wrung her hands in front of her. "I understand if you don't want me anymore." She lost her battle with her tears, and they poured down her cheeks.

He groaned and tugged her against his chest, his arms banding around her so tightly she squeaked. "Not want you?" He leaned back and captured her mouth in a kiss, backing her up until she was pressed against the wall, and they were the only two people who existed in the world. "Not want you?" he rasped again, as he leaned away and stared into her eyes, his hands playing through her hair and caressing her cheeks. "I'll want you forever."

"Niall," she cried out, arching up to kiss his jaw. "I'm sorry. Forgive me."

He kissed her again, more slowly, but just as passionately. When he broke the kiss, he backed away, but continued to hold her hand. "I need to understand, Hett. I need to know why you ran." His gaze shone with pain. "I'd never hurt you, and to think you didn't trust me ..." He shook his head.

"I saw you flirting with one of the Sirens," she whispered. "I thought it was really all a game to you—just after I'd realized I needed to be brave and to trust in you. I thought my heart would break."

"Oh, Hett," he breathed, dropping his head to rest against her shoulder. "Never. I smile and wink at all the women there, but nothing more. I promise."

At the knock on the door, Niall looked over his shoulder to see Da poking his head in. "Da?"

"It's time to come for supper. The other lads will cover the saloon tonight, and those who are free will celebrate Hettie's return to us." Seamus smiled at her, relief shining in his gaze.

Niall nodded. "There's so much more we have to say."

"Later," she whispered.

He nodded again, nearly falling to his knees in thanksgiving that he'd been granted another chance. That he stood with Hettie in his arms. That she'd returned to him. Linking his hand with Hettie's as they followed Seamus, Niall knew they'd find time alone, somehow.

Just as they were about to enter the O'Rourke house, and he knew pandemonium would break out as his mum and Winnie caught sight of Hettie, she tugged on his hand. Looking down at her, she stood on her toes and whispered in his ear, "Meet me in the kitchen tonight. When it's quiet. So we can dance in the moonlight." She lowered to her feet and bit her lip, waiting to see what he would say.

His breath caught. She had received his last gift. It had meant something to her. Grinning at her, he lifted her hand to kiss it. "Always, Hettie. Always."

~

Hettie walked hand in hand with Niall into the O'Rourke house, using the front door. All the unease and anxiety she'd felt in the pit of her stomach since she'd departed for Helena was gone, and she felt relaxed and like she was exactly where she was meant to be. She was home.

Casting a furtive glance at Niall, she knew that wherever he was would be home for her. There was still so much to say, and she didn't know if he truly forgave her yet, but she'd find a way to earn his forgiveness. She had to.

The time away from Fort Benton had taught her an important lesson. This was her family, and this was where she belonged. Niall was the man she loved and adored.

Standing near the entrance to the kitchen, Niall heard Maggie talking with Dunmore, Winnie, and Mary. "Won't you tell us your surprise?" Maggie asked.

Hettie exchanged an amused grin with Niall, as they listened in. She detected the delight in Maggie's voice at having Dunmore home, and they heard Dunmore chuckle.

"No. It's not my surprise to tell," he teased, and then Maggie shrieked, and Hettie imagined her husband tickling her. She heard a child giggle and clap, and Hettie suspected their two-year-old son, Lorcan, found their antics amusing too.

"Come," Niall whispered, squeezing her hand and leading the way into the kitchen.

Hettie watched as Niall beamed at his mum and then focused on the three women in the room, who were like sisters and a beloved aunt to her. Biting her lip at the hushed silence, Hettie felt a momentary panic that she'd been wrong. That she wouldn't be welcomed back by all the O'Rourkes.

A half second later, Niall laughed and released her hand, as Winnie squealed, Mary pressed a hand to her heart while tears formed, and Maggie jumped away from Dunmore to race to Hettie.

The women circled Hettie, holding her close and whispering in her ear. Although she couldn't make out everything they said around her quiet sobs, she felt treasured and loved. Looking over Winnie's shoulder, as she held her best friend close, Hettie saw Niall watching her and smiled at him.

She was home. She was safe. She would find a way to mend things with Niall. For she couldn't imagine a life away from him or his family.

Focusing on Mary, who stroked a soft hand over her head, Hettie smiled at the woman who she'd felt a near-instant affinity with since her arrival.

"Tell me that you were treated well, lass." Mary's hazel eyes shone with worry.

Hettie nodded. "I was. I'm fine." She smiled in Dunmore's direction, seeing him muttering soft comments to Niall, and shrugged. "Somehow Dunmore found me in Helena. I don't know how he knew to speak with Bailey and then to seek me out, but he did. And he brought me home."

Mary gazed deeply into Hettie's eyes, and whatever she saw eased her concern, as she squeezed Hettie's arm and backed away. "Yes, home, Hettie, my girl."

Maggie pushed forward and hugged Hettie, rocking her in her arms, and whispered in her ear, "I'll help you in any way, if you need it."

Hettie frowned, as she puzzled through Maggie's cryptic comment. "What? Oh, no!" she gasped. "I'm fine."

Maggie did the same as her mother, staring deeply into Hettie's eyes. She grinned mischievously, when she nodded in satisfaction. "Good." After winking at Hettie, she backed away and left Hettie with Winnie.

"Winnie," Hettie whispered, suddenly battling tears. "I didn't know if I'd ever see you again."

Staring at Hettie with relief and a touch of anger, Winnie swiped at her eyes. "You didn't leave me a note. You didn't say goodbye, Hettie." She bit her lip and then blurted out, "How could you? I thought I was your best friend."

Ducking her head, Hettie closed her eyes, as shame momentarily washed over her. "I know. I'm sorry. I'm so sorry. I overreacted and ran away."

Winnie pulled her close, wrapping her arms around her. "I've done worse and been forgiven," she whispered. "I'm so relieved you're well. And you're home." She eased away, tears leaking out. "I'm so happy you'll be here when our baby arrives."

Hettie gasped and squealed at Winnie's news, hopping up and down. "Everyone knows?"

Laughing, Winnie nodded. "Of course. We told them just after you left. It's why I'm so tired and crying all the time." She looked chagrined. "Everyone's been so good to me. Taking care of little Ava, cooking for us, doing all my chores. I'm being spoiled, and I haven't even had the baby yet."

"That's what family does," Hettie murmured.

Winnie nodded. "Aye, that's what *our* family does." Staring intently at Winnie, she murmured, "And you're part of this family, Hettie. No matter what happens."

Hettie nodded, her gaze drifting to Niall. She blushed when she found him watching her, although she was relieved to see the joy in his gaze. She prayed his delight in her presence never faded.

~

Later that evening Niall stood in the kitchen, staring out the back door, waiting for Hettie to arrive. Although the town wasn't as busy as when the steamboats came directly to town, the men who were here continued to make enough of a racket each night. Thankfully he was accustomed to their hooting and hollering and the random gunshots, although he yearned for the quieter season.

Closing his eyes, he dreamed of the time when they served a few of the locals each day, but kept much shorter hours, as both he and Lucien wanted to race home to their wives. He smiled as he envisioned returning home to Hettie. To her turning from the stove or raising her head from the back of the rocking chair where she'd been reading or sewing or doing whatever she wanted. His smile broadened at the thought of her working with him at the saloon and walking home with her.

"What has you smiling?"

He spun at her soft voice, his gaze flitting up and down as he studied her in the soft moonlight. She looked like an apparition, and he reached out, stroking a finger down her arm to ensure he wasn't in a dream. He shook his head, his eyes glowing as he looked at her. "Hello."

She stared up at him in wonder, as though she too were having difficulty realizing he were in front of her. "You're here," she whispered.

He chuckled and nodded. "Aye. I was lost to a waking dream, imagining what my life might be like, now that you've returned." He bent forward and kissed her gently. At her soft sigh, he broke the kiss and backed away. Taking her hand, he led her to the bench at the large kitchen table, pausing to stare at her for a long moment. "'Tis a bit cool tonight to sit on the back steps."

"I'd like to cuddle up next to you, as we stare at the stars."

He froze, gazing at her in hopeful confusion. "Truly?" At her nod, he took a step closer and lowered his head to hers. Closing his eyes, he rested against her for a long moment, savoring this time with her. "I can't believe you're here. In my arms."

Her fingertips played over his jaw. "I know."

Easing back a few inches so he could look into her mesmerizing brandy-colored eyes, he sobered. "I have to ask, Hett. Why did you come back? Was it for me or for my family?"

"What?" she whispered, her hands dropping away from him. She attempted to back up a step, but he kept his hands looped around her waist and matched her movement. "How can you ask me that?"

Swallowing, his breath fanned over her cheek, and he shrugged. "I saw you with them tonight. I saw how delighted you were to be back. How you wept with joy as they welcomed you home."

She stared at him in horror. "You don't believe in *me* anymore, do you?" Huffing out a mirthless laugh, she backed away again, and he let her, his hands falling to his sides. "How ironic. First I was the one who had trouble having faith in you, and now it's you with no faith in me." Her gaze shone with sadness. "We're doomed, aren't we?"

He watched her eyes filled with tears, as he hesitated before answering. "I hope we aren't," he finally said in a soft voice.

"No!" she cried out, striding the two steps toward him that separated them and hitting him on his chest. "No! You're supposed to fight for me and me for you and never doubt how much we love each other." Tears coursed down her cheeks, as she sobbed. "I love you so much, and I nearly lost you. Don't make me lose you now."

"Hett," he breathed, hauling her close, his face buried in her lilac-scented hair. "Hett," he breathed again, as his arms quivered. "You love me?"

Pressing back enough so she could meet his gaze, she smiled, standing on her toes so she could kiss his cheek. "Yes. I love you. So much." A tear leaked out, and she grinned at him.

He gave a small *whoop*, lifting her up and twirling her around. "I, … I can't believe it."

"Why?" she murmured, holding him close. "I've loved you since I arrived but knew I shouldn't."

He stiffened and pushed back, framing her face with his large callused hands. "Why not?"

"I'm the hired help, Niall." She spoke in a flat voice, as though her tone would take away the sting of the words.

"You know we don't care about that, Hett. *I* don't care about that." He froze when he saw the doubt and pain that lanced through her gaze. "Hett?"

"I *heard*, Niall." She raised a hand to his chest to keep him from tugging her close to soothe her pain. "I heard you and Lucien and Declan chatting the night of Bryan's party. I know how your family really feels about me."

"What?" Niall asked, leaning forward as his eyes blazed. "What do they really feel?"

"That you could do no worse, but that you could probably do better." She nodded when he froze, his gaze distant, as though reliving that moment. "That I was good enough, although Declan didn't see why you'd have to settle."

"No. Hett, it wasn't like that." Niall grabbed her arm and tugged her close. "Please, listen. Declan was trying to rile me up, to force me to realize that I was in love with you. His plan worked, but I didn't realize what I felt for you until a day or two later, when I saw you with that weasel. It's not about you *not* being part of the family. It's about facing up to you being *my* family, but not in a brotherly way. For I don't love you like a brother, Hett."

"You don't understand how those words devastated me." Her eyes glowed with the hurt and mistrust from what she'd overheard that day. "I had no one in my life when I arrived. I knew I was ... nothing."

"Don't say that," he snapped, before frowning. "You had Winnie." Tilting his head to the side, he frowned.

"I knew better than to expect more than to be the hired help."

"Dammit, Hett!" He cupped her face, his thumbs tracing over her cheeks. "You know I've never thought of you like that." His gaze bore into her. "I've never treated you like that."

"I'm an orphan, Niall. I don't have the right ..."

He placed his thumb over her lip and shook his head. "You can't blame yourself for being an orphan, Hett. And you can't blame me for a conversation you didn't understand." When she remained quiet, he whispered, "I've been so miserable." His hands stroked over her face and head, cupping her cheeks as he tilted her face, so she met his gaze. "I thought you would never come back and that I'd be the bitter uncle that his nieces and nephews dreaded visiting."

She fell forward into his chest, wrapping her arms around him. "Oh, Niall. I'm sorry. I should have been brave and confronted you." She let out a shaky breath. "I'd only just realized how much I cared about you, and then I saw you flirt and smile with the Siren."

Frowning, he urged her away so he could look into her eyes. "Hett, you know who I am. You know me." He waited, his tension easing as she nodded. "I might have flirted with her, but only because I was bein' kind. You know Da would never allow any of his lads to go to a place like the Bordello."

Hettie shrugged. "I hoped, but I never wanted to assume." Whispering her thanks as Niall handed her his handkerchief, she swiped at her cheeks and nose.

"Will you give us time, Hett, to rebuild what we lost?" Niall asked, his thumb playing with hers as they held hands. At her confused smile, he whispered, "Trust. Faith in tomorrow." He let out a shaky breath. "For, with you here in my arms, I'm learning just how much faith I have."

CHAPTER 15

H ettie entered Seamus's office, fighting fear and uncertainty. She had never been summoned to see Seamus, and he'd always been supportive, but in a distant sort of way, except for the time he visited with Jacob. Why did he want to see her now?

Hettie stilled, freezing at the sight of Declan and Lucien. She looked frantically for Niall, but he was nowhere in sight.

"You're well, lass," Seamus murmured. "There's no need for you to panic, and Niall's needed at the saloon. Can't have both of the older brothers away, leavin' the runnin' of it to the two wee rascals." He spoke of Bryan and Henri with deep fondness. "Come. Have a seat."

Hettie knew she looked like a frightened rabbit, but she did as she was bid, sitting in the chair across from Seamus and between Lucien and Declan. She gripped her hands together, her gaze flitting from one to the other. "I know you must have your doubts about me."

Holding up his hand, Seamus interrupted whatever else she might have said. "Nay, lass, stop right there. I fear you've misunderstood my lads, and we wanted to clear somethin' up." He looked at his two sons.

"Why isn't Niall here?" She bit her lip, after blurting out her question.

Looking at her compassionately, Seamus murmured, "You

wouldn't have had as much faith in what they said if Niall were here. I thought you'd feel they were forced into tellin' you what they must to clear the air." He grinned at her. "An' I'm not forcin' them either."

She looked at Declan and Lucien, fidgeting, because she knew these two O'Rourkes were the ones who disapproved of her the most. Fighting the pain of that knowledge, she met their concerned stares. "There's nothing to say."

Declan leaned forward and shook his head, with Lucien rising to stand beside his brother, so Hettie only looked in one direction. "That's where you're wrong, lass. I realized when I spoke to Niall this morning at breakfast that you still believe he could have done better than you." He flushed and shook his head. "I believe the opposite. You're his match. Like Lorena is mine."

She gaped at him and shook her head. "I don't understand."

"*Oui*, you do," Lucien argued. "Haven't you ever been frustrated when someone's taking too long to do something, so you give them a push?" He grinned at her. "We knew Niall was crazy about you, so we acted like we disapproved."

Declan chuckled. "And he acted like the overprotective, lovesick fool we knew he would." He frowned. "Only you didn't hear that part. You only heard the part where we goaded him."

"Truly?" Hettie whispered.

Reaching forward to clasp her hand, Declan smiled at her. "You're already our sister, Hettie. I couldn't be happier you've returned. Now Niall has a chance for what we have."

Hettie nodded, snatching her hand away to cover her face as she burst into tears. "Forgive me," she gasped, missing the concerned look shared between Declan and Lucien.

Seamus rose, crouching beside her to pull her into his strong arms. "There's a lass," he murmured, patting her on her back, as he rested her head on his shoulder. "You're loved by all of us, although not nearly as much as by Niall." His teasing earned him a soft chuckle from her, and he smiled. "Come. Dry your tears."

"I never thought to be worthy ..."

Lucien made a sound of disgust in his throat, while Seamus shook his head. "Nay, none of that. You've been worthy of our love and regard since you arrived. You're loyal and kind and good. You're one of us, Hettie." Swiping at her tears, he smiled softly at her. "When you left, you didn't only hurt Niall. You hurt us all. Thank you for coming home, lass."

Hettie nodded. For this was truly her home, and she felt welcomed.

Now, all she had to do was find a way to ensure Niall understood that she would never leave again and that their future was secure. To do that, she knew she had to share her deepest shame with him, which would take all of her courage. For Niall, she would try.

That evening Niall sat on the back stoop of the big O'Rourke house late at night, after closing up the saloon first. It had been a good day, although long. The incessant pain of missing Hettie was gone, although the persistent doubt that something more could occur to rip her away from him continued.

When the back door opened, he expected to hear his mum's soft voice calling out to him. Instead he calmed at Hettie's presence, as she nestled beside him, resting her head on his shoulder, as she tugged a blanket over her lap. "Hett," he murmured, kissing her hand and wrapping an arm over her shoulders.

"I've missed you," she murmured, pressing her face into his neck and breathing deeply. "Somehow I've missed times like this, even though we've never had them."

He smiled, kissing her head. "You had the dream of them, like I did, and missed them."

"Aye," she whispered, teasing him, as she added a soft Irish lilt to her voice. "I met with your da, Declan, and Lucien today." Running a hand over his chest, she felt him tense beneath her, and she held him close.

"What did they say?"

She pushed away to gaze into his eyes, although that was difficult as the moon was only a sliver, and there was little light on this dark evening. "Nothing to frighten me away." She blushed. "I realized I'd misunderstood everything. And that we'd always become so distracted by other topics when we spoke that I never listened when you said I'd misunderstood the conversation I overheard."

She scooted so she could cup his cheek and could peer up at him, even if she couldn't easily see his expression. "I never listened, Niall. I never heard. And I'm so sorry. I was deaf due to my fears, and I hurt you."

He nodded, turning his head to softly kiss her palm. "What did they say?" he breathed again, but this time the question wasn't laced with as much fear.

"That they were delighted I'd returned. That they were happy I was with you. That there was no better woman than me for you." She sniffled, suddenly battling tears.

Now Niall cupped her face between his hands, his thumbs brushing over her delicate skin. "That they were goading me into action because I'd been a dithering *eejit* for too long."

"Yes." She turned her face into his reverent touch. "I misunderstood everything and almost ruined what we could have. I'm so sorry, Niall."

He nodded, lowering his head so his forehead rested against hers. "I know you are, lass. You came back. You returned to me."

Taking a deep breath, she whispered, "Now it feels like you've left me. The part of you that was optimistic and determined? He's gone."

Groaning, he hauled her close, wrapping her in his arms. "He's not gone, Hett. That part of me's scared. I know what it is to lose you now. I don't know how I'd survive it again."

Clinging to him, she dug her fingers into his back. "You won't lose me. Not again. I'm here, and I won't leave you. I promise."

He held her, wanting to believe her words, but knowing he needed time to prove what she avowed to be correct.

CHAPTER 16

A week later Hettie turned to find Niall watching her. She
wished it was the way she used to catch him staring at her—
with a twinkle of mischief in his gaze and the hint of what would
blossom between them. Instead there was fear and uncertainty, before
he pasted on a smile that failed to hide his anxiety.

Approaching him, she kept her gaze locked with his and cupped
his face. "What is it?" She shook her head when he tried to twist out of
her hold. "No, Niall, trust me." She winced, as she knew there was
every reason for her to have lost his trust.

After a prolonged pause, he spoke in a soft voice that cut worse
than any yelling would have. "I'm wondering how long you'll stay
with me before something I do or say frightens you away again."

"Niall," she whispered, stepping forward to wrap her arms around
him. She squeezed him tight and then released him to gaze into his
eyes again. "I'm not leaving. I promise."

He nodded, but she knew he had little faith in her words.

"Are we doomed because you'll never fully trust me again?" she
whispered in a small voice. "Is this it?"

His hands gripped her so tightly that she gasped. Realizing he'd
unintentionally hurt her, he murmured an apology and tried to back

up a step. When she matched his retreat, he paused and continued to look into her eyes. "We aren't doomed, Hett." He swallowed and closed his eyes, shutting her out from what he was feeling.

She wanted to beg him to talk to her, but she bit her tongue, understanding she had to give him space. Give him time to regain his belief in them again. In her again. How had she been such a fool? "I'm sorry," she whispered.

"So am I," he said in so soft a voice she almost didn't hear him. He shook his head to ward off any of her protests that he had nothing to apologize for. "I'm sorry that I need time, Hett."

She nodded, her arms now wrapped around her belly. "How much time?"

He groaned and rubbed a hand over his face, before spinning and pacing away from her. "I don't know. I …" He shrugged and breathed, "Time. That's all I know I need."

Staring at his back, she waited for him to turn around and to smile at her. To give her some reassurance. To act like the Niall she'd loved and known before she ran away.

Instead he stood staring out a window, as though he'd forgotten she were here.

In that moment, Hettie realized all she'd jeopardized by not trusting in Niall. By feeding her fear and running from what they had. Would they ever recover what they had?

Niall left the saloon and wandered to see Mr. Pickens. Although Niall was much closer to Da and Declan, Niall felt an affinity with the older man because he doled out wise counsel in time of need.

Knocking on the door, he smiled when A.J. answered. "Hi, Mr. A.J." Niall rubbed at his head and shrugged. "I'm not sure why I'm here."

"You're here 'cause you're actin' like a pea-brained idiot." He motioned for Niall to join him on the porch, where two rockers waited for them. "More comfortable out here than in our cramped house."

After settling into the rocker with a sigh, A.J. lit his pipe and took a deep puff. "And I get to have a few puffs." His brown eyes gleamed, as he stared at Niall. "You over your mad yet, sonny?"

Niall grinned at being called "sonny," something, until today, which had been mainly saved for his older brothers. Then he shrugged and answered A.J.'s question. "I think I am, and then I think about her leaving again, and I'm filled with a red rage." He formed a fist with one hand, tapping it into the palm of his other hand. "I don't know what to do to rid me of it."

A.J. sat in his chair, rocking comfortably. "*Hmm*, I wonder." He met Niall's perplexed stare and shrugged. "You got to get over your mad at yourself first. You were the idiot who let another man woo your woman. You were the one who risked losing her. You were the one who didn't race after her."

Niall sighed and ducked his head. "She wouldn't have wanted me to."

"From what I've heard from my Bessie, an' she's a wise woman …" He paused, as though waiting for Niall to disagree. When Niall nodded his head in agreement, A.J. gave a grunt of pleasure and puffed on his pipe again. "My Bessie tells me young Hettie was miserable from the minute she was on that stage coach."

Niall leaned forward, resting his arms on his thighs. "How does she know that?"

"Womenfolk. They talk better than us men do." A.J. shrugged. "Except for me. I tend to chatter worse than an old widow." He grinned as Niall rolled his eyes at him. "Your brother Bryan takes after me." He looked as proud as any father at the thought.

"Now you've got a choice, sonny. You can keep your anger as your bedfellow, or you can make your peace and have your woman beside you." His brown eyes were suddenly devoid of all humor, as he gazed at Niall with complete seriousness. "You can't have both."

Heaving out a sigh, Niall bowed his head forward, rubbing at the back of his neck. "How do I let go of it?" Raising his head, he looked at A.J. beseechingly. "How do I overcome it?"

His expression filled with compassion and understanding, A.J.

murmured, "Ah, lad, you know how. You watch what your parents did. You see that love and faith and hope is always worth more than fear and pain and anger."

"Faith," Niall whispered.

"Trust in her," A.J. murmured, "or she will never fully trust in you."

Niall returned to the saloon, relieved and determined to find a way past his fear and doubt. Thankfully it was a slow day at the saloon, and he had plenty of time to think about Hettie, without being too friendly to customers. With a sigh, he remembered his vow to believe in actions as much as words. Hettie had shown him how she felt and had said it. He'd thought his heart would leap from his chest at her avowal of love. Somehow he had to overcome his fear.

After serving a customer, he focused on Bryan chattering to Henri, smiling, as they were fast friends, like Niall was with Lucien. Niall also liked to listen in on Bryan's ramblings because he always learned something about someone in town or someone in the family. Somehow Bryan was a fount of knowledge. Smiling, as he realized Bryan had just referred to Hettie, Niall dried a glass and focused on tidying Bryan's end of the bar.

"So then I said to Mum, if she's leavin' again, could I have her room? That way, we'd have more space, and the three of us wouldn't be crammed into one room." Bryan paused as Henri muttered something to him and then laughed, punching his brother on his shoulder. "No! I get her room!"

Niall froze as he tried to understand what Bryan had said. Hettie was leaving again. What? "Bry?" He spoke in a soft voice, but it held the command of an older brother. He jerked his head, and Bryan was at his side, swiping his palms over his pants leg. "Who's leavin'?"

"Hettie, of course," Bryan said, with a bright smile.

Shaking his head, Niall hissed and rapped his fingers on the bar. "Watch my side, eh?" He ruffled Bryan's brown hair and slipped from the saloon. Although Niall attempted to corral his anger, he knew it was a futile endeavor.

Hettie planned to leave again? Was she going to tell him this time or sneak away yet again? A red rage overcame him.

The thoughts swirling through his mind repeated over and over. Hettie was packing again. Hettie was leaving him again. After being teased with heaven, he'd lose her again.

Bursting into the café kitchen, he saw her working peacefully with Deirdre, their harmonious song ending precipitously. Looking like a madman, with his eyes blazing and his cheeks flushed, he hissed, "You're leaving?" His focus was solely on Hettie. On the guilt that flashed through her gaze. On the way she flinched at being caught.

"What?"

"Wee Bryan told me that you're packin' and leavin'!" He gripped his hands into fists, ready to grab her, so she couldn't leave him again.

Transforming in front of him, she faced him, her cheeks reddening and her eyes like molten honey as she glared at him. "You listened to him chattering away, and you believe what he had to say?" Her gaze shone with disappointment and sadness. "You'll never trust me again, will you?"

"Answer me!" he roared. "Are you leavin' me again?" Unable to hide the anguish in his voice, he held his fists at his side to prevent them from shaking. He stood, in a quagmire of uncertainty, longing, and pain, as she stared at him like she didn't know him.

When she finally whispered, "No," he let out a deep breath and bent forward at the waist, as though he'd just run a long race. "Thank God."

"You'll never forgive me, will you?" She stood bravely in front of him, as though a criminal awaiting her punishment. "You'll never put behind us what happened." A tear coursed down her cheek. She shared a quick glance with Deirdre, who nodded, and Hettie raced away, her footsteps sounding on the stairs to the second floor.

"Hett," Niall breathed, racing after her to the large living space over the café. He stilled when he saw her crumpled on the sofa, sobbing quietly. Standing at the entrance to the living room, he murmured, "I will get over you leaving … because you came back."

"It's not enough though, is it?" she whispered. "I abandoned you, and you'll never forgive me."

He moved to her, sitting beside her. He hated how she flinched as he gently touched her leg. "And *abandoned* is a harsh word. You left, and you came back." He swallowed, hating how his voice broke. "I'll find a way, Hett. I promise."

She sat as in a trance, rocking in place. "I abandoned you. I betrayed myself." She sobbed, as she bent forward at her waist, her shoulders heaving with her sobs.

"Hett?" he whispered, moving to kneel in front of her. "What is it?" By this point, she was lost to her grief, curled over herself, incapable of hearing him. He eased her off the sofa so she sat on the floor in his arms, his heart breaking as her words had changed to "Please don't abandon me."

"Never, my Hett. Never." He kissed her head and stroked her back, rocking them in place. "I'll never abandon you. I'll cherish you forever."

Her crying jag abated, and she brushed her face against his chest, swiping away her tears. "You can't mean that," she stammered out. "You can't cherish me and mistrust me, Niall."

He closed his eyes, a sigh brushing against her soft curls. "I know, my love. I know." His hold on her tightened. "Why would Bryan say you're leaving?"

She sniffled and pushed away from me. "Because I am." She shook her head at the pain she saw in his gaze. "I'm leaving your parents' house. I'm moving in here."

"Why?" he rasped, cupping her face.

"There's been talk." She flushed and ducked her head. When he tilted her head up for him to look into her eyes, she closed them. "Talk about us and impropriety and …" She bit her trembling lip, as more tears leaked out.

"And?" Niall rasped.

"And that, now that I'm a ruined woman, you don't need to marry me because I'm living in your parents' house, and you have easy access to me."

Niall froze, his eyes now molten with fury. "Who?" he rasped. When she remained stubbornly quiet, he asked again, "Who would dare say such a thing?"

"Janet Davies," she whispered.

"That witch!" Tugging Hettie into his arms, he held her close, breathing in her subtle scent of soap and lilacs. He buried his face in her hair, silently chastising himself for having jumped to the wrong conclusion and for hurting her again. For hurting them. How would he earn her trust when he continued to prove his lack of it? "Forgive me, Hett?"

She sniffled and looked down at the floor. "I can't continue on like this, Niall." She clung to his shoulders, as she sat in defeated misery in front of him. "I'm sorry for what I did, but I can't go back and change what happened."

Cupping her face, he nodded. "Be patient with me. Please, Hett." He swallowed. "I ... There are things you need to know. Not today. Today, sit here with me for a few more moments, before returning to help Deirdre. Tomorrow, go walking with me?"

She nodded, nestling against him. "Yes, Niall."

He sighed, thankful for this moment with her, but dreading discussing his youth with her. However, he knew he had to tell her about Colleen, if he ever hoped to have any harmony in his relationship with her.

CHAPTER 17

The following evening Lucien had pushed Niall out of the saloon, so he could search out Hettie. Niall knew he'd promised to speak with her, but he was terrified. He knew she would be at his parents' house that evening, and so he headed home, so they could go on their promised walk.

Rounding the corner for home, he paused at the sight of her sitting on the back steps, her head tilted up to the warm rays of the late-evening sun. A soft breeze blew her honey-blond hair, as it lay in soft curls around her shoulders, and a gentle smile lifted her lips. He'd never seen her so beautiful.

"Hett," he murmured, hating how she froze and watched him guardedly, before offering a hesitant smile. Reaching out his hand, he spoke in a soft voice. "Will you walk with me?"

He wanted to howl and scream at her hesitant nod, knowing he'd been the one to rob her of her bloom. Her joy. He wished their companionable camaraderie continued, but he felt tongue-tied and like a foolish lad, so he remained quiet. Holding her hand, they walked in silence a short distance from town, past Declan and Lorena's bookstore and to a place that curved toward the bluffs, bracketing the backside of Fort Benton.

"Why here?" She stared up at him in confusion, as she knew the family always wandered to the spot by the creek.

"This is a place many of us men come to when we need to work out our frustrations but don't want our womenfolk to know. We scream and yell and holler and throw rocks. I've been coming here a lot lately." He sighed when he saw the hurt in her gaze. "And I knew they'd come looking for us at the creek. I want time alone with you for a bit."

At her nod, he settled on a boulder and waited for her to do the same, smiling when she sat primly. "It's all right to relax, Hett. It's just the two of us." He reached out a hand, relaxing a little when she reached back, so their fingers were touching and tracing each other's.

"I have to ask you a question. It's eating me up inside, and I'm sorry." He release her hand as he rose and paced, kicking at small rocks. "I have no right, but I have to ask." His green eyes blazed, as he came to an abrupt stop, staring at her like she was the only thing on this earth he saw. "Did you allow ..." He shook his head. "Did he ..." He broke off and spun away, muttering a swear word as he rubbed at his nape. "I have no right to ask."

He stilled when he felt soft fingers tracing the rigid muscles of his back. "Did I ever do anything more than kiss Jacob?" she asked in a soft voice. "Is that what you're trying to ask me?"

He spun and faced her, his eyes ablaze, as he nodded. "Aye." He nearly panted with frustration and fear, as he waited for her to answer.

A tremulous smile spread, and she shook her head. "Of course not, Niall. I only ever dreamed of you. I only ever wanted you." She raised a hand to press her palm against his cheek. "I, ... I did kiss him, but it felt like kissing a brother. Nothing like the nights we kissed."

"Like I'd die if I didn't hold you in my arms and kiss you," he whispered.

She bit her lip, her eyes now glowing too. "Aye," she teased, then squealed as he tugged her into his arms. "I've missed you so much."

"Ah, Hett, I've been goin' mad with jealousy and knowin' I had no right." He grunted when she hit him on his arm, and he backed up a step.

"If you have no right to it, then who does?" She shook her head, as though perplexed. "I'm not sharing you either, Niall. You're mine."

Grinning down at her, he traced the little furrow between her eyes that occurred when she was fierce and chuckled. "You're claimin' me, are you?" At her nod, his smile softened. "Good, lass. I want the same." He sobered and took a deep breath. "Will you listen? I have to tell you something, and then, then we can decide where we go."

She clung to his hand and sat on the large rock so they were side by side, although she sat in such a way where she could look into his eyes. "Whatever you tell me, darling, won't change how I feel. Or what I want."

"What do you want?" he whispered, his voice husky.

She paused, and it looked like she was gathering all her courage. Just when he thought she wouldn't answer his question, she said, "To be with you forever."

"Ah, lass," he rasped, leaning forward to kiss her. "So brave. So determined." He squeezed her hand. "But hear me out first, aye?"

She nodded, squeezing his hand back.

"Mary's not my mum, aye?" When she nodded, he heaved out a breath. "Colleen was my mother. She was ..." He paused, as images of the woman who'd raised him the first twelve years of his life flashed through his mind. A few fleeting moments of laughter and joy nearly drowned out by screaming, sorrow, and rage. "When I think of my mother, all I feel is her misery. She hated her life. Hated me most of all because she thought I'd ruined her life."

"Niall," Hettie breathed. She bit her tongue, as she knew he needed to speak these words, but they hurt her. Oh, how they tore her to pieces.

He ducked his head, but not before she saw the shame he was unable to hide from her. "Aye, she told me often enough. That, if I'd not been born, then perhaps Da would have loved her. That he'd been tied to her and resented her because of me." He closed his eyes, his shoulders tense. "Or, if she hadn't had me, she would have had the courage to leave. I'd anchored her to her misery. And I was a wee bastard to have …"

Hettie covered his mouth, her eyes overflowing with her tears, as she shook her head and looked at him. "No! No, Niall. Don't repeat her foul, offensive words. They're lies." Her voice broke, as she pleaded with him to believe her. "Lies!"

"My own mother didn't want me, lass. Why should you?"

Hettie launched herself at him, the force of her movement making him grunt and knocking the air out of him. "No!" she screeched and sobbed. "No!"

"Hettie, love," he murmured, "don't cry."

Clinging to him, she kept her arms wrapped tightly around him, as she pressed her head to his chest. "Have you thrown rocks and yelled and screamed at her here?" she stammered out. "You must let her go, Niall. Let her lies go."

"Hett," he breathed, burying his face in her hair that was coming free from the loose bun. His fingers dug into it and into her back, holding her close. "I never blamed you."

Pushing against him and wriggling until he eased his hold on her, she backed away so she could meet his gaze. Her hair tumbled free in disheveled waves, and her eyes were blotchy from her tears, but she didn't care. All she cared about was him. "For what?"

He lifted a shoulder, appearing embarrassed.

"No," she said in a low growl, her brandy-colored eyes shimmering with her fervent belief. "You believe in me, as I believe in you. You believe you're worthy of my love. As I am yours." Her fingers gripped his shoulder to the point she nearly bruised him. A tear coursed down her cheek, and her voice was *stuttery*. "Or we truly are doomed."

"I love you, Hett," he whispered. Rather than the proud or defiant declarations of the past, this was a quiet avowal of his deepest truth. "I always have."

She nodded, another tear leaking free. "I love you too. I always have."

He swiped at her face, marveling that she had cried for him. She had wept at the thought of his mother mistreating him. Her sorrow was for *him*.

He'd heard her words, and they'd filled him with joy, but her actions filled him with hope. Her actions proved her declaration was so much more than mere words. "Marry me, Hett."

She gasped, staring at him in confused wonder. "You want to marry me?"

He smiled at her, its tenderness causing her breath to catch and more tears to form. "Of course I do." He let out a deep breath, as he cupped her face. "I was afraid. Of what you'd think when I told you about my mother." He swallowed. "Of how you'd react."

She stepped even closer, so they were pressed, chest to chest. "You worried I'd agree with her?" Her gaze shone with compassion. "Never."

His smile softened, and his hand slid over her cheek, so his fingers teased the sensitive skin below her ear. "I'm not afraid now."

A brilliant smile burst forth, and Hettie threw herself into Niall's arms. "Yes! Yes, I'll marry you, Niall."

He groaned, lifting her up and twirling her around, before hollering out, "Yes!" When he set her down, he captured her lips in a passionate kiss, breaking away when he knew he wouldn't want to stop.

Staring into her delighted gaze, he understood how fortunate he was to have been given a second chance, and he'd do everything he could to never risk losing her again.

Leaning against him for a moment, she whispered, "Should we tell your family, or should we wait a little while?"

A tiny bit of his joy faded at her wording of that question, and he cradled her face in his hands, his thumbs playing over her cheeks, as he stared deeply into her eyes. "*Our* family. And, yes, let's tell them. I want to share our happiness with them. I'm proud of you. Of us." When she smiled so brightly that it was like she sparkled, he hauled her close. "I love you, Hett. We'll be so happy."

～

As they approached the large O'Rourke house, Niall's grip on her hand tightened, and he squeezed it. "Why are you fidgetin', Hett?" he murmured. "They'll be delighted we've finally come to our senses."

She turned, pressing into his chest. "I ... There are things you don't know about me, Niall. I have to tell you ..." Her voice broke, when Kevin called out to them to quit dawdling and to join them inside. She closed her eyes in defeat.

Niall leaned away, his focus wholly on her. "We can go anywhere right now, and you can tell me. Or we can wait to share our news." He frowned, as he traced away a lone tear on her cheek.

"I don't want to wait." She shook her head in frustration. "I'm bursting with joy and pride and all these emotions that you want to marry me. I won't be able to keep it a secret." She ducked her head to hide her abashed smile, but met his gaze when he made a sound of disappointment that she was hiding from him.

Another tear leaked out. "You shared your deepest truth with me, Niall, and I haven't been so brave. I ..." She bit her lip and stuttered out a breath.

Taking a tiny step toward her, he leaned forward and pressed his forehead to hers. "Whatever you tell me, whatever you believe shameful, I promise you, Hett, that nothing will prevent me from wanting to marry you. Trust me."

She let out a shaky breath, tilting her head so she could kiss him softly. "I do."

He waited, ignoring everything around him but her. His hands caressed up and down her back, reveling in giving her comfort, as he waited for her to decide what she wanted them to do.

"Can we tell them tonight and talk tomorrow?" She arched back to look into his eyes. "I wish I were still living here. I could meet you in the kitchen tonight."

He groaned, his hands gripping her close, as he kissed her softly. "No, it's better you're at Ard's. Now that we're engaged, I don't want any more gossip to ever harm you, Hett." He released her and reached for her hand again, giving her a soft smile, as she leaned close to him.

After walking inside with her, he smiled at his family. He knew they would have all eaten supper by now, but Mum would have saved some for him. Thankfully Lucien, Bryan, and Henri were at the saloon, and he'd have to return there soon. But, for now, he'd relish this short time with most of his family. He only wished they were all together.

As the family conversation quieted, when he and Hettie remained standing, he grinned at all of them, before focusing on his mum and da. "We're to marry."

He shrugged at making such a simple pronouncement, but he didn't know how else to tell them. In the end, it didn't matter, as they let out a roar of delight and swarmed around him and Hettie, hugging and kissing them.

His mum pulled him close, her arms squeezing him tight. "Oh, my sweet lad, I'm so happy for you." She backed away and whatever she saw in his eyes made her smile. "Be happy."

"I am," he whispered.

"Good." She grinned at him. "I know you love having the entire family around you, but marry soon, lad. Don't waste any more time."

He grinned at her, watching as Hettie laughed and cried while speaking with Maggie and Winnie, and nodded. "Don't worry, Mum. We'll wed soon."

"Good."

CHAPTER 18

The following day Hettie slipped out of the café during a lull between meals to go to the saloon to see Niall. The prior evening's events seemed like a dream, and she wanted to see him to reassure herself that they'd really occurred. She was marrying Niall. She would have her heart's desire.

With a spring in her gait, she sidestepped a few men having a heated discussion and continued toward the saloon. When a hand grabbed her arm, she gasped at the pain and the shock of someone reaching for her.

Glaring at Mrs. Davies, Hettie battled an instinctual desire to flee from her. For some reason, this woman had an ability to cut her to her core with words. "Let me go!" She wrenched at her arm but only managed to cause Mrs. Davies to latch on even tighter, like a vise.

Janet Davies leaned toward her, shaking her head. "Oh, no, you harlot. I'm not letting you go until I take you to where you belong." She tried to drag Hettie behind her, but Hettie dug in her heels, and neither of them moved. Finally Janet looked at her, staring at her with blatant pity.

"Let me go!" Hettie repeated, kicking out and hitting the older woman in the shin with her booted toe. At the woman's shock of being kicked, she released Hettie's arm, and Hettie backed away. "Don't speak to me! Don't touch me."

"Oh, you think you're so precious now, don't you? Now that you believe he'll marry you." she cackled. "He won't marry you. And, if he does, he'll leave you when he realizes you're nothing. You're nothing but an unwanted, worthless orphan."

She gloated when she saw Hettie flinch at her words. "Keep lying to yourself, sweetie. Just like my Aileen. She's lied to herself for years that her husband really wants her. But he's miserable with a wife who can't give him a child. Just like yours will be with you because you're nothing but trash."

Biting her lip to keep it from trembling and to prevent a sob from bursting forth, Hettie spun on her heel and walked to the saloon. She wanted to run, but she didn't want to give that horrible woman the delight of seeing her flee from her. Leaving without muttering a single retort was bad enough.

Entering the saloon through its back door, she attempted to regain her composure. Realizing she was failing as Bryan took one look at her and raced to find Niall, she remained in the small rear room, not wishing to smile and fawn over customers. When Niall burst into the room, she threw herself into his arms. "Hold me," she whispered.

"Always," he breathed, his hands digging into her waist, as he held her closer and then even closer still. "You're well, love. You're well."

"I have to tell you something," she whispered. "I ... Before you hear it from someone else." She quieted, battling a fierce sense of rejection when he whispered, "No." Squirming in his arms, she tried to break free. "I'm sorry. I shouldn't ..."

"Hett," he murmured, "I want to hear what you have to say but not here. Give me a minute to talk with Luc, and we'll go." He backed away, looked deeply in her eyes as he ran a finger down her cheek, and was gone.

Feeling bereft, but clinging to hope and her courage, Hettie waited for him to come back. Within a minute, he was reaching for her hand and leading her from the back of the saloon, down the steps, and to the café. Soon, she was upstairs, in the living room, pacing.

"This won't do," Niall muttered, striding toward her and pulling her close. "Whatever you have to tell me, all will be well, Hett. Let me hold you, and you can say anything."

She shuddered and clung to him, as they stood with her cradled against his chest. "I know it's scandalous, but will you hold me? ... Hold me as we rest on top of my bed?"

He huffed out a soft laugh. "Ah, you want to cuddle with me," he teased. "Of course I'll hold you, love." He released her and followed her to her new room here at Ardan's, his hand resting lightly on her shoulder.

With the door shut, the distant sounds of the café and the town were like from a dream, and they were in their own little world. Niall had kicked off his boots and rested on his back, stretching his arm out, so she would lie against him.

"Come, love. It's like when we're out by the stream and looking at the clouds. Lay your head on my shoulder."

She tumbled onto the bed and curled into his side, only this time, she wrapped an arm around his waist and pressed her head against his chest. "I love you," she whispered.

"And I you, Hett. What happened to chase the joy from your beautiful eyes?"

"I ran into Mrs. Davies today." Tears spilled down her cheeks, and she pressed against him, taking comfort in his silence as he waited for her to speak. "She taunted me. She pricked at all of my old fears."

Niall sighed, his hands running over her shoulders and back. "She always tries to find what will hurt the most and strikes there. 'Tis the way of a bully, Hett. You should give her no mind."

She sniffled and nodded, her grip on him not easing. "Aye, I know you're right, but it's hard when she pokes at your worst fears."

After long moments of silence, punctuated by his steady breaths and the soft sound of his hands tracing over her back, he murmured, "Won't you share them with me?"

Pushing up on her hands, she lifted up enough to look into his eyes. "I have to tell you who I am." Swallowing in a hope to steady her voice, she said, "You need to know who I am."

He frowned, running a finger through her golden locks. "You're Hettie. Henrietta Foyle, an orphan from England. I don't need to know more."

Tears seeped out. "No. I'm Henrietta Foyle. The girl no one wanted. The girl whose mother and father abandoned as soon as the ship landed after the crossing. Too expensive and cumbersome to be worth the bother."

She spoke with a crispness and a precision to her language, as though mimicking what had been said to her all those years ago. Taking a stuttering breath, she continued, "The girl who had to lie and steal and cheat to survive." She swallowed. "The girl who was so desperate, she almost had to do the unthinkable."

He studied her intently before breathing, "Almost."

Nodding, Hettie stared at him with shame and misery. "I was on the verge, ... on the verge of visiting a place like the Bordello, when I met Winnie." Swallowing a sob, she rubbed at her eyes. "Winnie saved me, as much as the O'Rourkes did, and I abandoned her the minute I arrived here, desperate for a job."

Niall gazed at her, wide-eyed and stunned, as though attempting to puzzle through everything she said. "Hett," he breathed, his fingers still slowly stroking over her. "You didn't abandon Winnie or her friendship. We put you in a terrible position of having to choose." He swallowed. "I never understood until now what that choice was."

"Mrs. Davies believes I belong at the Bordello. Perhaps she's right," Hettie whispered.

"No!" Niall rasped, his grip on her tightened, as though battling images of his precious Hettie at the Bordello. Rolling so he leaned over Hettie, as though sheltering her with his strong body, he added, "No, never, my darling Hettie." He swallowed as he pushed down a nearly overpowering rage, while he struggled to ease her of this torment. "Your parents?" he whispered, still struggling to understand what had happened to her.

She reached up, running her hand over his shoulder, as though reassuring herself of his strength and presence. "I told Winnie that they died on the ship passage here to America. It's the lie I've told myself and anyone who asks because I'm so ashamed of the truth." She closed her eyes as though to hide that shame.

Taking a deep breath, she opened her eyes and bravely met his patient, loving gaze. "However, the truth was so much worse than that. They left me on a street corner, with nothing more than the clothes on my back, telling me to wait for them. That they'd be back after they found a place for us." She closed her eyes, as tears leaked out. "I was so stupid. I waited and waited, even when it got dark, and I was so cold I thought I'd freeze. I fought the police who pushed me off the corner, saying I had to move on."

"Did you ever see your parents again?"

"Never," she whispered. "I ... survived. People had more sympathy for an orphan than a child discarded, like a piece of trash."

He cradled her face, his green eyes glowing with passionate devotion. "Never talk like that about yourself, Hett. Never."

She nodded, as more tears leaked out. "They left me. Without a second thought."

Niall nodded, his gaze protective, as his jaw clenched and unclenched. "That's what you're most afraid of." He looked at her for a long moment, as though figuring out a puzzle. "Being abandoned again."

She nodded.

He made a small motion with his head; his cheeks were flushed, and his green eyes shone with frustration. "You believed I'd abandon you."

Her eyes filled with more tears, and she cried out, "My own parents didn't want me, Niall. My own mother walked away and didn't look back." She closed her eyes in an attempt to blot out that memory. "They left me to starve. How could I believe in your constancy?"

His caress on her cheek was light and reverent. "And now?"

She shrugged. "Now I can't bear to not hope and dream."

He nodded and looked away, his shoulders tight and jaw clenched, although his touch remained gentle. "Why?"

Frowning, she paused as she thought over their conversation.

"Because I've seen how your family is. I've seen how everyone struggles and fights and works to stay together. To support each other. To forgive hurts and disappointments and to never give up." She swallowed, blurting out, "I've heard the story, again and again, of Mary's return. Of your father's joy. I know what he felt now."

He frowned, staring at her intently. "What do you mean, lass?"

"It's how I felt when I saw you again, and I'd only been away from you for a few weeks. The overwhelming joy and relief and love. I can't imagine years." Tears threatened again, and she battled terror at feeling so vulnerable. When he remained quiet, she raised a hand, tracing a furrow between his brows. "Maybe I'm a fool ..."

He shook his head in silent inquiry when she broke off what she would have said.

"Maybe I'm a fool for believing ..."

His eyes lit with love and devotion, and he smiled for the first time in what seemed like forever to her. "Oh, no, Hett, you ain't a fool. You never have been." He turned his face into her fingers, as they tracked down his cheek, kissing them.

Taking a deep breath, he spoke in a low, fervent voice. "This is what I know to be true." He waited until she gazed deeply into his eyes. "You are not a hardship. You are not a bother. You are priceless and precious and—" His voice broke, as he yanked her to him. He shuddered as he held her, burying his face in her neck, while he battled fierce emotions and a sob. "I want to strangle them for ever hurting you and for making you feel less than worthy of my love. Of my family's love. I hate imagining what could have happened to you."

"I had to earn love. Don't you see?" she whispered. "I had to make you see I was worthy of—"

He covered her lips with his, breaking off whatever more she would have said that would further break his heart. "No," he rasped, as he broke the kiss. "No, love." He peppered kisses down her neck. "You have always been worthy of my love. Of all of our love."

Easing her away so she rested on her side again, he leaned over her with his gentle caresses stroking up and down her arm and over her shoulder. "'Tis why you felt the need to work and work, to prove yourself worthy of our love?"

She nodded, her gaze shattered and filled with shame.

"You know I feel the same, my love. You know it, after we spoke near the cliffs last night." He paused. "Why not tell me then?"

"I was trying to work up my courage, and then you said you wanted to marry me." Her eyes bright with the wonder of that, she trailed a finger through his hair. "I, ... I needed at least a night to believe I was worthy of you."

"Hush," he murmured, kissing her softly. "You wouldn't let me talk that way, and I won't let you either. We both knew heartache, Hett. And now we'll only know joy." He kissed her again. "Even when we argue, I never want you to believe I'll wish for someone other than you. I never want you to think I'll leave. I'll never leave you."

She continued looking into his eyes, her gaze filled with trust and devotion. "I realize now I ran because I was afraid. I thought you couldn't love me, and so I would abandon you before you could me."

He groaned before kissing her again. "That'll never happen, Hett. Never."

She smiled, her expression filled with her belief in him, before biting her lip. "I don't want secrets between us." He nodded, and she felt a further lightening of her spirit. "Janet ... bruised me again."

"What?" he growled, his hands playing over her wrists and up her arm as he watched her closely to see where she winced. When she jerked away when he touched her near her left elbow, he pushed her sleeve up. "*Jaysus*," he rasped, his fingers tracing over the reddened area. "This will bruise terribly."

"Yes. She was angry." Hettie fought a sob, as he continued to trace his hands over her as though his soft touch could ease her of all the pain caused by the older woman's brutal touch. "I didn't want you to think you'd done something to hurt me in case you touched me there in the next few days."

He nodded, his green eyes smoldering with rage. "No secrets, Hett." At her nod, he muttered, "Then you should know I'll speak with her." When Hettie simply nodded, some of his tension eased. "No one hurts you, Hett."

She tugged at him, and he tumbled to his back, so she could snuggle against his shoulder. "Five minutes more before we have to return to work."

"Ten," he breathed, holding her close.

CHAPTER 19

The following morning Niall entered the laundry—a hot, humid space, with clothes on drying racks near a stove pumping out heat even on this hot day—and nodded to Howard, the owner, before focusing on Janet Davies scrubbing away in the back. "I need a word with Mrs. Davies." Howard motioned for him to wait outside, and Niall nodded.

He stepped out onto the boardwalk, thankful for the reprieve from the stifling heat inside, and took in deep lungsful of the relatively cooler air. How could anyone stand to work there?

Turning to face Janet Davies when he heard her footsteps, he stood tall, unable to hide his glower.

"I wondered if she'd cry like the weakling she is to you."

"Don't," Niall barked, the word spoken in a lethally low, cold voice. "Don't speak of my intended. Don't think of her. Don't look at her." He took a step closer to the older woman, meeting her defiant stare with a murderous glare. "If you ever touch her again, if you ever taunt her again, you'll be on the next stagecoach out of this town, away from here."

"You wouldn't dare!" she hissed.

"Oh, I would," he murmured, his gaze glinting at having the upper hand. "I know you receive more deference than you should because your niece is married to my brother," Niall said, referring to Aileen, his brother Kevin's wife. "You'd have nothing if you left this town."

"I can speak the truth to anyone I want," she protested, her hands on her hips, only highlighting the threadbare clothes she wore.

"Ah, but you never speak truth though, do you? You only speak what you know will cause the most pain and agony." Leaning away from her, he was silent a long moment before he said, "No more mischief. Not with Hettie. Or anyone associated with the O'Rourkes."

She snarled at him but spun on her heel and stormed back inside to work.

Letting out a deep breath, Niall turned and looked around. Although he wished he could yell at Mrs. Davies more, he knew he'd said all he could. He paused when he saw the Madam watching him, and he strolled toward her, attempting to appear calm and collected, although he was still itching for a fight. "Madam Nora."

She smiled at him and looped her hand through his arm, as though they were out for a morning stroll. Maneuvering him so he walked her by the Missouri and away from the men loitering around town, she murmured, "Did you take care of your problem?"

"I believe I did."

She squeezed his arm. "Good. I had heard she'd hoped to convince young Henrietta to join me." She raised an eyebrow, her brown eyes filled with disdain. "As if that woman could manipulate me into accepting Henrietta as a Siren."

Niall paused, his gaze troubled. "Hettie admitted she'd been on the verge of such a life. When she was desperate before she came here." He cleared his throat. "If Hettie had come to you, of her own free will ..."

Nora looked at him sorrowfully. "I would have hoped you had as much sense as your brother Finn did, when Winnie was faced with the same choice. Few women are as fortunate to be adored by someone like the men from your family."

Niall nodded. "Thank you, Madam Nora, for your friendship. To me and to my family."

She smiled. "Always." She squeezed his arm, and they started walking again in a circuitous route back toward the Bordello. "Don't forget to invite me to the wedding. I love weddings. And cake."

He chuckled, agreeing with her request. After leaving her at the Bordello to return to work, he felt lighter in spirit. Mrs. Davies knew better than to approach Hettie again, and Madam Nora, a formidable champion, was looking out for Hettie too. Niall could ask for no more.

~

"Let's get married in a week," he murmured on a rare free afternoon from the saloon, two weeks after they'd announced their engagement. They'd walked a short distance upriver to a quiet area and lounged on the riverbank on a blanket under the shade of a cottonwood.

Resting on her belly, she leaned on her elbows and peered down at him. "A week? That's fast, Niall."

He traced a pattern over her cheek and shrugged. "I know, love, but I'm tired of snatching moments with you. If we're married, at least I know I'll be holding you in my arms at night. I know I'll see you every day for more than five or ten minutes."

She smiled, her gaze filled with delight, as she lowered her head a little and bit her lip. "So you're saying you miss me."

He grinned at her flirting with him. "You know I do, you wee witch." He reached over, tickling her and laughing like a kid, when she squealed with delight and tried to squirm away from him. Soon she was laughing and crying and calling out, "No more!" and he hauled her against him, holding her close to his chest. "Ah, how you brighten my days, Hett."

"And you mine," she gasped, as she regained her breath and settled against him. "I never thought I could be this happy."

He kissed the top of her head, delighted to see her hair a disheveled mess, as he frowned. Reading between the lines of what she didn't say, he murmured, "You deserve it, love." He felt her take a deep breath and then relax against him even more.

"I do," she whispered. "I do deserve this." She leaned back and met his gaze, smiling impishly. "Let's marry in one week. I can't wait to be your wife."

Gaping at her, he swallowed, unable to speak. Finally he whispered, "Really? You'll marry me so soon?"

"Yes. I want our life to start now. I'm tired of waiting. No time will be perfect." She bit her lip. "But where will we live?"

He sighed and groaned. "I don't know. I don't want to live with Ardan or my parents. I want us to have our own place."

She ran her hands over his chest and sighed. "There aren't many men coming in now. Maybe we could claim one of the rooms over the saloon as ours?"

He grabbed her hand and raised it to his lips. "Let me talk to Da." After kissing her fingers, he rested back, holding her close. "For now, let's enjoy this moment. Knowin' my family, the minute we tell them we want to marry in a week, it will be chaos."

She giggled and snuggled closer, and he sighed with pleasure to simply hold her in his arms, as a deep contentment filled him. Soon he'd marry the woman of his dreams. He could want for nothing more.

Hettie moved around her bedroom at Ardan and Deirdre's, packing up her belongings. In two days, she and Niall would wed. In two days, she would move to their new home. Smiling to herself, she knew something was occurring at the saloon, but she had been forbidden from entering the saloon since the afternoon she and Niall had spent by the river.

Sighing, she folded a skirt to place in her bag, and looked around her room. Although she'd only been here a short while, this had been a comfortable room, and she would be forever grateful to Deirdre and Ardan for giving her a place to stay.

"Might I come in?" Mary asked, poking her head in.

"Of course." Hettie smiled at the older woman and then her breath caught, as she realized Mary would be more than a woman she considered a benevolent aunt. Against her will, her eyes filled with tears, and she was suddenly unable to speak.

"Lass!" Mary cried out, rushing to her. "Are you well? Do you need Niall?"

Shaking her head, Hettie collapsed onto a chair by the window. "No, I had a thought that shocked me."

Mary paled, gripping her hand, as she perched on the edge of the bed. "Please tell me it wasn't something that would keep you from marryin' my Niall."

Hettie jerked her head and met Mary's worried gaze. "Of course not." She flushed and whispered, "I realized I'll be like Aileen and Deirdre to you now."

Mary frowned, her hold on Hettie's hand tightening. "I don't understand, love. What do you mean?"

Hettie sighed and leaned forward, rubbing at her temple. "I'll be family, so you'll have a reason ..." She broke off, biting her lip.

Mary murmured a sound of protest, as she stroked a hand over Hettie's head. "So I'll have a reason to love you?" At Hettie's nearly imperceptible nod, Mary sighed. "You're wrong, you know."

Hettie flinched, forcing herself to look at Mary, as Hettie was unable to hide the devastation in her gaze. When she tugged on her hand, desperate to rise and flee, Mary held on to it and shook her head.

"I already love you like a daughter, Hettie. Marryin' my Niall changes nothing for me, except that now it's official. Finally everyone in town will understand you're an O'Rourke, as you have been since you arrived in Fort Benton."

Hettie huffed out a breath, failing to swallow an ungraceful sob. Instead it burst forth, and she fell forward, as Mary wrapped her in her arms, with deep keening wails pouring from Hettie.

Through it all, Mary held her, rocking her in her arms and murmuring soft words of understanding and caring. "There's a love.

There's my Hettie," she murmured. "All is well. You'll not be alone again."

"You know?" Hettie stammered out.

"Aye, Niall shared your story with me a few evenings ago, when I met him in the kitchen, while I was getting my glass of milk." She stroked a hand over Hettie's tear-stained cheek. "His story about his mother's lack of love is too much like your own story. Yet Niall and you've always been wanted by us, Hettie." Her hazel eyes shone with sadness and a fierce devotion to her. "I'm so sorry you suffered as you did, but so thankful you came to us."

Hettie rested her head on Mary's shoulder. "Me too." After a few more long moments she whispered, "That's what I realized when you entered the room tonight. You could be my mum. I could have a mum again." Another tear trickled down her cheek. "I haven't had a mum in so long."

"Ah, Hettie," Mary murmured. "I'd be honored."

Hettie rested her head on Mary's shoulder, as the realization hit her that all her dreams were coming true.

CHAPTER 20

Hettie smiled shyly at Seamus as she met him in the café kitchen. Although she didn't want to keep Niall waiting, she needed another moment to compose herself, as her nerves threatened to overwhelm her.

"You're well, lass?" he murmured.

She smiled at him. "I am."

"Good," he said, as he spoke in a soft voice. "I couldn't be prouder that you'll finally be my daughter. I've never seen Niall so happy—or so at peace. Thank you, Hettie."

Her eyes filled, and she blinked rapidly. She didn't want to cry today. She wanted to laugh and celebrate and feel joy. "Thank you, Seamus."

He squeezed her hand and gave her an expectant look.

After she took another deep breath, she nodded, and they walked out the café door, away from the bustling part of town, toward the slightly quieter area, near where Lorena and Declan had their bookstore and school. Seamus had constructed a simple one-story church a few years ago, and Niall waited for her inside, along with the rest of the family and the priest.

As she approached the church doorway, Hettie took a deep breath to calm her racing heart and nerves. Glancing down the aisle, she saw the priest at the altar, Niall waiting for her, Lucian by his side. When Niall cast furtive glances in her direction, she wanted to race to him. Suddenly any doubts and fears vanished, and all she wanted was Niall.

Beaming at him, she walked beside Seamus toward Niall, her focus wholly on the man she loved, who would be her husband. His green eyes shone with pride and delight, and her breath caught as he grabbed her hand, lifting it for a quick kiss.

"Hett," he breathed, "you're a vision."

Running a hand over the beautiful dress all the O'Rourke women had worked on, Hettie smiled. "As are you, my Niall." Barely focusing on the priest, they spoke their vows at the appropriate times, although their gazes never wavered from each other.

Finally Niall bent forward to kiss her, a soft, reverent kiss. When he backed away, she flushed and gripped his hand. "Soon," he murmured, running a finger over her cheek, beaming at her when she flushed and nodded.

After greeting everyone outside the church, he walked with her back to the café, where a huge feast awaited them. Soon the newlyweds were separated, as the family and close friends surrounded them. After more hugs, kisses, and words of congratulations than she ever thought possible, Seamus cleared his throat, and everyone quieted. Hettie moved to stand beside Niall, her head on his shoulder, as he wrapped an arm around her, holding her close.

"Aye, 'tis a grand thing to see us all together today and for such a wonderful celebration. Niall and Hettie, you knew hardship before you met, but you didn't allow the bitterness and the disappointments of the past to ruin your chance for love. You've shown courage and faith and love. Qualities you will need every day in your marriage."

Raising his glass, he spoke in a strong, sure voice. "May you always have the surety of the love you feel today."

A soft roar of agreement rose from the O'Rourkes, with a nod from Nora too, and Hettie pressed against Niall as she felt Seamus's blessing. She trusted that, whatever was to come, she and Niall would face it together, strong in their love and in the love of the family that would unfailingly support them.

～

Giggling, Hettie entered the empty saloon and looked around in wonder. She'd never seen it so quiet on a summer night. "I can't believe it was closed."

Niall grinned at her. "It's closed for three nights. One of Da's wedding presents for us."

She gaped at him, as she covered her mouth in wonder. "Three nights?"

Niall nodded. "Aye. He wanted us to have time without listenin' to loud and rowdy men downstairs."

"It's something we'll have to accustom ourselves to," she murmured, wrapping her arms around him. "I can, as long as that means I'm close to you." She kissed his jaw. "I hate being away from you, Niall."

"Ah, Hett," he breathed. "I know a saloon isn't a proper place for a wife, but …" He paused, cupping her face and kissing her for a long moment. After breaking the kiss, he whispered, "Do you think you could be happy with me?"

She grinned at him. "I know I can." She pressed against him. "Show me the surprise you've been working on."

He flushed and motioned to a space behind her. "There's one over there, but the main one's upstairs. Come." He gripped her hand and led her up the stairs. He grinned when she gasped at the door at the top with a sturdy lock on it.

"Niall?" she whispered.

He reached into his waistcoat pocket for the key and unlocked the door. Then he led her inside. "I know I haven't been with you as much as I'd like this past week. But I was busy …" He stopped speaking when she covered her mouth again and stared around with wide eyes.

All of his brothers and his da had worked every evening—and sometimes all night—so that it would be done in time. Although it still smelled of fresh paint, the entire upstairs had been transformed again. Although two bedrooms remained, they were freshly painted, and the other rooms had been transformed into a large living area for them. "This is our home," he whispered, when she remained quiet.

"Oh, Niall!" she squealed, throwing herself into his arms. "I never thought ..." She released him to trace her fingers over a couch and moved around the space, as though in a trance. "We have a home of our own."

"Aye," he murmured. "There's no kitchen up here, but we put one in downstairs. It's small, but it works."

She spun and launched herself at him again. "Oh, my Niall. Thank you."

He held her close. "Anything for you, Hett," he murmured, peppering kisses over her cheek. "We can ... We can make it work ..."

"Kiss me, darling," she whispered. "We've waited so long."

He leaned back to stare into her beautiful eyes. "I don't want to rush you."

A brilliant smile burst forth, and she shook her head. "We've waited four years. That's long enough."

Niall groaned and hauled her close, kissing her with unrestrained passion. "Too bloody long," he moaned, backing her to the bedroom and to find the passion within.

～

Hettie rested her head on Niall's shoulder, her fingers tracing over his chest. "Only three days?" she murmured. When she felt his chest rumbling with laughter, she flushed and giggled.

"Don't worry, love. The slow season starts soon." He kissed her head and yawned, holding her close. "So you enjoyed it?"

Pushing back, she gazed down at him in the vague light of only one candle. Her hair was a tumultuous mess, falling in riotous waves down her back. Unable to tease him, she grinned shyly at him. "Yes." She looked away, only meeting his gaze again when his fingers stroked over her cheek. "Did you?"

He smiled; his green eyes lit with joy. "Aye, my Hettie. You're my dream come to life." He lowered and kissed her softly. "I'm glad we didn't marry until the slow season was upon us. I want all the canoodling time we can get." When she flushed, he chuckled. "There's no need to be embarrassed, love. All the O'Rourkes enjoy their canoodling time."

"I know," she whispered. "I never thought to be so lucky." When her stomach growled, her eyes widened with embarrassment. "Ignore it!"

He frowned, his thumb rubbing her eyebrow. "Ignore when my wife is hungry?" Shaking his head, he rose. "Give me a minute." After slipping on his pants, he left, returning a few short minutes later with a huge plate of food, including a massive slab of wedding cake.

"Where'd you get all that?" Hettie asked, as she sat up and reached for a fork. "We shouldn't eat in bed."

"We can do what we want, Hett," he said, kissing her. "We'll deal with the crumbs later. For now, eat."

She devoured the food she'd been too nervous and too excited to eat at their wedding celebration, enjoying chatting with Niall about the day. "How was there food downstairs?"

"Mum and Deirdre promised they'd sneak in with food. They'll leave it in the kitchen downstairs. Deirdre whispered she'd bring over food tonight too, as she remembered nearly starving on her wedding night." He grinned at Hettie, as she giggled.

"What was Oran talking about with Bryan and Henri?" Hettie asked, after swallowing another bite of cake. She played her fork's tines through crumbs, as though debating eating any more.

"Open," Niall murmured, gently feeding her another bite. "Oh, Oran has it in his head that he'll never meet a woman. He's trying to talk the other pack members into sending away for mail order brides."

"They're too young to be worried about marriage!" Hettie sputtered.

Niall shrugged. "Lucien married young and is happy. And they're not wrong. 'Tis rare to meet a fine woman in the Territory. We O'Rourkes have been uncommonly lucky."

She leaned toward him, kissing him soundly. "Aye, you have been."

Niall set aside the plate of food and tugged her into his arms. "Promise me that we'll always be this happy."

Twisting so she could look into his eyes, she shook her head. "No, Niall. We'll be even happier."

W ant More Niall and Hettie? Sign up for my newsletter for a bonus epilogue, just for newsletter subscribers- like you!

SNEAK PEEK AT PIONEER VALOR!

What happens when the mail order bride arrives, and she's not the woman he wants?

Oran O'Rourke has lived a charmed life as a member of the esteemed O'Rourke Family in Fort Benton, Montana. He's lived life to the fullest as a member of the pack, running wild and creating mischief with his younger brothers. Now, his only unfulfilled dream is to marry, and find happiness as his older siblings have.

Against all advice, Oran sends away for a mail-order bride. Finally, she is to arrive as the steamboats begin sailing up river. However, what is he to do when the woman he sent for isn't the woman he desires?

Preorder Pioneer Valor Now- Coming in February 2023!

ALSO BY RAMONA FLIGHTNER

The O'Rourke Family Montana Saga

Never fear, I am busy at work on the next book in the series! If you want to make sure you never miss a release, a special, a cover reveal, or a short story just for my fans, sign up for my newsletter!

Follow the O'Rourke Family as they settle in Fort Benton, Montana Territory in 1860's.

Sign up here to receive the prequel, *Pioneer Adventure* to the new Saga as a thank you for subscribing to my newsletter!

Pioneer Adventure (Prequel)

Pioneer Dream (OFMS, Book 1)- Kevin and Aileen

Pioneer Desire- (OFMS, Book 2)- Ardan and Deirdre

Pioneer Yearning- (OFMS, Book 3) Niamh and Cormac

Pioneer Longing (OFMS, Book 4)- Eamon and Phoebe

Pioneer Bliss (OFMS, Book 5) Declan and Lorena

Pioneer Devotion (OFMS, Book 6) Maggie and Dunmore-

Pioneer Ardor (OFMS, Book 7) Lucien and Samantha

Pioneer Redemption (OFMS, Book 8) Finn and Winnifred

Pioneer Delight (OFMS, Book 9) Niall and Hettie

Pioneer Valor (OFMS, Book 10) Coming Spring 2023!

Bear Grass Springs Series

Don't worry, I am busy at work on the next book in the series! If you want to make sure you never miss a release, a special, a cover reveal, or a short story just for my fans, sign up for my newsletter!

Immerse yourself in 1880's Montana as the MacKinnon siblings and their extended family find love!

Montana Untamed (BGS, Book 1) Cailean and Annabelle

Montana Grit (BGS, Book 2) Alistair and Leticia

Montana Maverick (BGS, Book 3) Ewan and Jessamine

Montana Renegade(BGS, Book 4) Warren and Helen

Jubilant Montana Christmas (BGS, Book 5) Leena and Karl

Montana Wrangler (BGS, Book 6) Sorcha and Frederick

Unbridled Montana Passion (BGS, Book 7) Fidelia and Bears

Montana Vagabond (BGS, Book 8) Jane and Ben

Exultant Montana Christmas (BGS, Book 9) Ewan and Jessamine

Lassoing a Montana Heart, (BGS, Book 10)- Slims and Davina

Healing Montana Love (BGS Book 11)- Dalton and Charlotte

Runaway Montana Groom (BGS, Book 12) Peter and Philomena-

Substitute Montana Bride (BGS Book 13) Tobias and Alvira

Enraptured Montana Bachelor (BGS Book 14) Cole and Wilhelmina

Fervent Montana Devotion (BGS, Book 15) Shorty and Rose

Reluctant Montana Husband (BGS, Book 16) Coming October 2022!

The Banished Saga

Follow the McLeod, Sullivan and Russell families as they find love, their loyalties are tested, and they overcome the challenges of their time. A sweeping saga set between Boston and Montana in early 1900's America.

The Banished Saga: (In Order)

Love's First Flames (Prequel)

Banished Love (Banished Saga, Book One)

Reclaimed Love (Banished Saga, Book Two)

Undaunted Love(Banished Saga, Book Three) (Part One)

Undaunted Love (Banished Saga, Book Three) (Part Two)

Tenacious Love (Banished Saga, Book Four)

Unrelenting Love (Banished Saga, Book Five)

Escape To Love (Banished Saga, Book Six)

Resilient Love (Banished Saga, Book Seven)

Abiding Love (Banished Saga, Book Eight)

Triumphant Love (Banished Saga, Book Nine)

Are you feeling Daring?

Ramona writing as Fiona Cullen, sexy small town romances set in beautiful Montana! (warning, they are spicy, with open door sex scenes with swearing).

The Burkes of Burnside Creek Series:

Unexpected Montana Love (Prequel for Newsletter subscribers only)

Forbidden Montana Love (BBC, Book One) Nolan and Theo

Secret Montana Love, (BBC, Book Two) Chase and Ally)

Blazing Montana Love (BBC, Book Three) Coming November 2022!

NEVER MISS A RAMONA FLIGHTNER UPDATE!

Thank you for reading *Pioneer Delight*! I hope you enjoyed Niall and Hettie's story as much as I enjoyed writing it. Please consider leaving a review! Reviews help other readers take a chance on books, and they mean the world to me. Thank you!

I love hearing from you, so please feel free to write me and let me know what you think!

You can reach me at: ramona@ramonaflightner.com

Join My Newsletter For Updates, Bonus Scenes, and Sneak Peeks about the series you love!

Want new release alerts, access to bonus materials and exclusive give-aways, and all my announcements first? Subscribe to my weekly newsletter!

Want to be notified about freebies and sales? Try Bookbub!

Want to stay up to date on new releases, my life in beautiful Montana, and research trip adventures? Follow my hashtag #ramonasmontanalife to follow along with my adventures as I post gorgeous pictures and videos of my life in Montana. Find Me On Facebook! Or Find Me On Instagram!

ALL ABOUT RAMONA

Ramona is a historical romance author who loves to immerse herself in research as much as she loves writing. A native of Montana, every day she marvels that she gets to live in such a beautiful place. When she's not writing, her favorite pastimes are fly fishing the cool clear streams of a Montana river, hiking in the mountains, and spending time with family and friends.

Ramona's heroines are strong, resilient women, the type of women you'd love to have as your best friend. Her heroes are loyal and honorable, men you'd love to meet or bring home to introduce to your family for Sunday dinner. She hopes her stories bring the past alive and allow you to forget the outside world for a while.